I Never Asked
You to Understand Me

Nothing's Fair in Fifth Grade
Sixth Grade Can Really Kill You
How Do You Lose Those Ninth Grade Blues?
Seventeen & In-Between

I Never Asked You to Understand Me

A NOVEL BY

Barthe DeClements

Viking Kestrel

VIKING KESTREL
Viking Penguin Inc., 40 West 23rd Street, New York, New York 10010, U.S.A.
Penguin Books Ltd, Harmondsworth, Middlesex, England
Penguin Books Australia Ltd, Ringwood, Victoria, Australia
Penguin Books Canada Limited, 2801 John Street, Markham, Ontario, Canada L3R 1B4
Penguin Books (N.Z.) Ltd, 182–190 Wairau Road, Auckland 10, New Zealand

First published in 1986 by Viking Penguin Inc.
Published simultaneously in Canada

Printed in U.S.A. by The Book Press, Brattleboro, Vermont
Set in Sabon Roman
1 2 3 4 5 90 89 88 87 86

Library of Congress Cataloging in Publication Data
DeClements, Barthe.   I never asked you to understand me.
Summary: Two teenage girls attending an alternative
high school for problem students find that their
disintegrating family lives have pushed them to the edge.
    [1. Non-formal education—Fiction. 2. High schools—Fiction. 3. Schools
—Fiction. 4. Family problems—Fiction I. Title.
PZ7.D3584Iac 1986   [Fic]   85-40839   ISBN 0-670-80768-0

This book is dedicated to the students whose lives are a bit too hard and to Diane, who tries to keep them safe.

ACKNOWLEDGMENT

This book was five years in the making. Through the various versions and revisions, I had the help of family, friends, teachers, and students. I would especially like to acknowledge and thank the following people: Doug Strom, who worked with me on the party scene, and Greg Myers; my son Christopher Greimes, who worked with me on the band scene and took me to the Laserium at the Seattle Science Center; my daughter Mari Greimes, who gave me technical advice for the version with the heroine as a dancer; and my daughter Nicole Southard and her husband, Doug Southard, who typed the second revision on their computer.

My heartfelt thanks also to Karol Gadwa for giving me access to the students in the CLIP program. And those students, Dave Anderson, Jackie Capp, Jon Hammond, Scott Hoskins, Helen Sharp, Sherri White, and Caprice Yarnell, and their teachers, Gloria Hubacker and Karen Swaney, have my gratitude for their consultation on the third revision of the manuscript.

Diane Heck faithfully read each chapter of the original story, and she was the inspiration for Dianna. EJ Rimbaugh was the inspiration for the gentleness and wit of TJ.   B.D.

One

Leaning against the wall of the outer office, I waited for the milling crowd to clear out around the front desk. Transfer papers from Alderwood High to the alternative school hung from my hand. I watched as the principal opened the door of the inner office and frowned at the secretary. "Why aren't these kids in class?"

The secretary raised her palms toward the ceiling. "Good question."

"Steve," the principal demanded of the boy nearest her, "why aren't you in class?"

"I've been trying to go, Ruth, but I gotta get a pencil from Dianna first."

Dianna pulled out the top drawer of her desk. "Give me a dime."

"I ain't got a dime," Steve said.

"You haven't got a dime," the principal corrected, retreating into her room at the sound of a ringing phone.

"That's what I said," he called after her.

Jee-sus, this was going to take forever. I flipped my papers back and forth in my hand while Steve talked Dianna out of a pencil and then helped himself to the Reese's Pieces in the jar on her desk. As he went out of the office, he held the door open for a girl coming in.

The girl stopped uncertainly a minute before moving over to the wall next to me. I didn't say anything to her. I didn't know if she'd remember me, but I remembered her. Around Edmonds and Lynnwood, the kids who party end up bumping into each other at one stomp or another.

I'd bumped into her twice. The second time was at the party where her boyfriend lost it all over the place. I wondered what she had done to him out in the garden in the dark to make him scream so much. She seemed so quiet while we waited for the secretary to notice us.

"Can I help you girls?" Dianna asked.

"Uh, yes." I stepped forward with the girl following me.

Dianna took our papers and ran a finger down her list until she came to our names, Deirdre Neil and Stacia Reynolds. After she checked off our names, she looked up at me. "OK, Stacia . . ."

I pointed to my chest. "I'm Didi."

"And I'm Stacy," the girl added.

"OK, Didi and Stacy." Dianna nodded toward the office window. "The orientation room is through that blue door across the court."

Stacy and I walked over slowly. I hated the whole idea of being in this school. Stacy didn't look too happy, either. She flashed me one desperate glance before she opened the door.

We were barely inside the room before some asshole muttered, "Check out those ni-ice tits!"

I stopped dead at his desk. "How rude can you get?"

He just shrugged, and Stacy acted like she'd never heard. I guess she's used to it.

The teacher looked up from a bunch of orange cards he was sorting. "Take a seat anywhere, girls."

The chairs were scattered all over the room. Not in straight rows like in a regular school. Stacy and I pulled two of the chairs close together and sat down.

The teacher called the roll from his orange cards. The boy with the mouth was named Larry. He had black curly hair and held his head rigid while his eyes darted from side to side. The blond boy beside him was TJ. TJ was good-lookin' in a dropout sort of way, slouched down in his seat, staring out of stoned blue eyes.

The teacher started in on the rules. Like you couldn't bring drugs to school. You couldn't smoke cigarettes, except in the designated area. You had to go to class every day for the two-week orientation period. And you didn't get scheduled into regular classes until your two weeks' work was in order in a folder.

The teacher, who said his name was David, warned us not to skip any classes, and then he gave us a sheet with the school district rules and the school rules and told us to write one hundred words summarizing the rules.

Baby-sitting. I took my pencil out of my purse, read over the rules, and wrote a hundred words. That left ten minutes to sit there watching the other kids work. All of them except TJ. He scribbled down something fast and then sunk into his jacket like a turtle and closed his eyes.

The old grade school coat closets were behind TJ. They were stacked with magazines. Or once were stacked. Half the magazines had spilled onto the floor. Chunks from the ceiling were on the floor, too. I wondered if that was asbestos hanging between the broken laths. The school district obviously wasn't betting on us.

"I don't believe this," Stacy said. She was watching a girl reach under her seat for more paper. Her shirt was unbuttoned halfway to her waist.

"Culls," I told Stacy. "We're in a school for rejects."

Stacy didn't look like a reject to me, and I didn't think I did, either. We were just having too hard a time. I knew about my hard times, but I didn't know all about Stacy's. Not for a long while. Then, when I found out, it made me sick. I knew it happened to girls, but it still made me sick.

Anyway, we had to stay in the orientation room all day, and different teachers came in each hour. The second one was Madge. She was the school counselor, and even though she was old, she wore jeans like the rest of the staff.

I was expecting more rules or a ditto sheet and a bunch of groans. Instead, the kids who were in the school last year called out her name, and she smiled and called them by name. TJ opened his eyes and stretched up out of his jacket.

"TJ!" she said. "You're back again."

Madge sat on a desk and told us about Games People Play. She was pretty funny. She used kids in the class as examples of the games. Like "Cops and Robbers" and "Blemish" and "How Do You Get Out of Here?" and "Let's Pull a Fast One on Joey." She used Stacy as an example for "Divide and Rule."

She pretended Stacy had been partying every night and only came home to crash, dump her dirty clothes, and get clean ones. When Saturday night came, she wanted to borrow the car, but she knew her mother would be pissed because Stacy never cleaned the house or did the dishes or anything. So Stacy sat on the arm of her daddy's chair and told him how young he looked and how all her friends were amazed that he was old enough to be her father.

Then Madge asked the class if Stacy would want her mother to come out of the kitchen while she was asking her dad for the car keys. Of course not. That was the point, "Divide and Rule."

Stacy bowed her head while Madge was rattling on about sitting on her "daddy's" chair. I saw Stacy's jaw go stiff.

I think Madge saw it, too, but she didn't stop the story.

Madge told us people didn't need to play games if they had the courage to be open and honest. Counselors always talk about being open and honest. Just about as often as they ask, "And how do you feel about that?" But if you ever forget yourself and blurt out the truth, they swell up like toads.

When my mother was dying, Mrs. Kimpton asked me how I felt about my mother's having cancer, and I said I thought it was sad. And then, like they do, she asked me how I felt about *that*. I said I felt my mother was concerned about herself and wasn't thinking about me.

That was one of the times Kimpton swelled up. After she got herself together, she leaned across her desk and said in that sugary voice high school counselors use, "Now, Didi, I *know* your mother loves you more than anything in the world."

She didn't know anything.

We had to write our own example of a game when Madge was finished telling us hers. Madge walked around the room checking our papers. While I was writing, I kept hearing a bird twittering. I looked up several times, wondering where the sound was coming from.

The twittering kept going on. Finally Madge stopped in the middle of the room and said, "TJ!"

TJ pulled his jacket away from his shirt and peered down inside. "Ohh," he said in a horrified voice, "it shit in my pocket!"

The whole class laughed. Madge laughed right out loud. I'd like to see that in a regular school. A girl by TJ told him he'd better get it out of his pocket or it would get squished by his jacket.

Madge shook her head. "TJ!" And she went on around the room.

The third teacher's name was Ellen. That's what she said—Ellen. She had that scrubbed, smiley, I-love-everyone look of a born-again Christian. Right away the old kids in the class started pleading to play volleyball. "Come on, Ellen, we've been sitting here being good for two hours, give us a break, you're so nice and we've been working so-o hard."

"Well, all right," Ellen said. "If Joe can get the keys to the gym from the office."

Joe could get the keys to the gym from the office. Joe, TJ, and Larry set up the net. Ellen didn't do anything. She didn't even have a whistle. She just sat on the stage and talked to a pregnant girl who didn't want to play.

The kids sorted themselves on two sides, and the game started. Larry served first. "You'll never get this one," he hollered as he bammed the ball up to the rafters.

I laughed. Nobody else did. They just tossed him the ball again. The second time he kept his mouth shut and stared ahead intently, but it didn't help. The ball hit the net.

On my turn I was a little nervous. I'm just five feet one and a half, but I'm strong. I was nervous anyway and let my breath out with relief when my serve was good.

TJ returned it. TJ's thin, with wide shoulders and no hips, and he looked like an exclamation point, bending this way and that. Larry did OK after he settled down. Stacy did well, too. Even though she's top-heavy, she's coordinated. One girl was hopeless, but nobody said anything. They just backed off and let her try. After her third bad serve Joe caught the ball, held it, and yelled at Ellen, "How much more time?"

Ellen looked up at the clock. "Three minutes."

"Animal Ball!" Joe hollered, and zipped the ball to TJ. TJ smashed it back. Larry kicked it.

Stacy and I crowded up on the stage. We're coordinated, but not that coordinated.

At noon, tables were set up in the gym. The cook and a couple of helpers wheeled out the hot lunch carts from the kitchen. Stacy and I fell in together when it came time for lunch. We were lolling at the end of the line, comparing our former high schools, when Joe pushed on our backs.

I turned around. "What's the big hurry?"

"The big hurry is I'm hungry," he said.

"So-o?"

"So-o the first ones get the food."

"What about the last ones?"

"If the cook runs out, no food."

"Can't the cook count?" I asked.

"No, and she can't cook, either."

"Where's the food come from, then?" Stacy wanted to know.

"It's sent down from Fircrest High," the girl in front of me said. She was the one who didn't know how to button her shirt. I closed the space between us, anyway. I wanted to eat.

The food was the same as in any other school, but when I lifted my arm off the table to hold my milk straw, my sweater stuck. I jerked it loose and looked down at the line of goo on my sleeve.

"What a pigsty," I said to Stacy.

After lunch Stacy and I went to the "designated" smoking area. The area is an open courtyard (great in rainy Washington) surrounded on three sides by one-story classroom units. On the fourth side is a covered basketball court. Beyond the basketball court are woods going up the hill toward Fircrest High. The alternative school is in a sort of hole with a graveyard on one side and a hill on the other. Symbolic, I guess.

There are long logs in front of the art unit. Stacy and I sat on one and watched some of the kids throw a Frisbee in the open courtyard. Larry came up and tried to bum a cigarette. We told him we didn't smoke. TJ was coming toward us until he saw something under the covered area and veered off to the side. Larry saw it, too, and split in a hurry. I stood up and backed through the crowd to see what it was.

A bong. It was a bong being passed around. They didn't

even bother to move off into the woods like in a regular school.

I didn't see TJ again until we were back in the orientation room listening to Simon, the art teacher, explain how to make a paper folder to hold our assignments. TJ and Larry came in late, and Simon told them they'd have to make up eleven minutes. TJ sat down, sunk into his blue ski jacket, and fell fast asleep while Simon went on explaining how to design our folders.

"That school's unreal," Stacy said when we were walking out to the buses.

"TJ's cute," I said.

"Captain Ozone," Stacy said.

I nodded in agreement, but when I looked out of my bus window I didn't see trees and houses whizzing by. I saw TJ leaping for the volleyball.

Two

The next day was more of the same. Only Ellen didn't take us to PE. She gave us a test to see how we scored in math. And Madge gave us an attitude scale to see how alienated we were. Stacy and I ate our lunch with our elbows up. Fortunately for our health, the food was on paper trays. I watched for TJ, but I didn't see him in the lunchroom. He'd come to first period twenty-five minutes late, and David had marked that down on TJ's orange attendance card.

When school was over, I weaseled Stacy's and my exit from the orientation room so we'd be walking by TJ on the way to the buses. Out of the corner of my eye I saw

Larry cock his head toward us and say something to TJ. Larry and TJ moved in.

"Wanna go down to the beach?" Larry asked.

"What?" I said.

"Wanna walk down to Edmonds Beach with us?"

Stacy drew back a few feet. "I have to go home."

TJ raised an eyebrow at me. The bus driver honked and then honked again. I shrugged helplessly at TJ and climbed on the bus to mumble to myself. Why didn't I go with TJ and Larry even if Stacy didn't? What difference did it make? I hardly knew Stacy.

When my house came into view, I shut my eyes, blotting it out for a minute. On the porch, I took a big breath before I went in. Passing her closed door dropped a depression over my head like a shroud. Up in my room, my bears sat on the end of my bed. I took up Tender Love, the one that was special to me, and hugged him to my chest.

Whenever kids start bitching about their mothers, I have nothing to say. There was never anything to hate. She spoiled me, I guess. Like the bears. I'd asked for one for Christmas, but she gave me two because she couldn't decide which I'd like the best. Maybe things like that made me selfish.

The spring before I went to the alternative school, I had had all kinds of plans about what I'd get and what I'd do. In the summer, Mother and I were going to Mexico. In the fall, I was entering high school and was going to take three more years of French and Spanish and two years of

German. For my birthday I planned to ask for the foreign language cassettes that my black-eyed Spanish teacher recommended. I had secret fantasies about him that no one suspected until my great-grandmother came for an Easter visit.

It was during her visit that the lights first dimmed at the carnival and I was left swingin' at the top of the Ferris wheel. I remember I was curled up in a chair, spacing out, when my great-grandmother came into the living room and picked up the business section of the newspaper.

"You've been thinking of romance, huh, Deirdre?" she said as she settled down on the davenport.

I looked up, surprised.

"Your aura has a rosy glow, you know."

"I didn't know," I said, and put my arms protectively around my head while my great-grandmother laughed. That old woman always knows everything. Actually, I don't call her great-grandmother. I call her Grandmother like my father does. She's seventy-six years old, but she gets around.

My mother came in the room with her coffee cup, and Grandmother looked at her sharply. My mother noticed it and said nervously, "Too many cups of coffee?"

"Have you had a checkup this year?" Grandmother asked.

Mother sat down beside her. "No, but I'm due to get one this month. What do you think of your great-grandchild's being voted the best foreign language student in the ninth grade?"

My grandmother nodded and gave me a fond smile. She

went back to San Francisco after Easter Sunday. The next week, Mother had her checkup. Three days later, on the doctor's instructions, Dad took her to the hospital. He made me stay home.

I waited hours and hours for him to come back, and then all he told me was that he didn't know what was the matter with Mother, and to go to bed. I couldn't stop asking him, "What did the doctor say? Don't they at least know if it's serious?"

"I don't know anything. They don't know anything. Go to bed." He went into their bedroom and closed the door.

I walked around the living room feeling lonesome and scared. I called my friend Adel. It was late at night and her mother answered.

"Is something wrong, dear?"

"My mother's in the hospital."

"Is it serious?"

I gave up trying not to cry. "I don't know. Nobody will tell me. Can I talk to Adel?"

"Would you like us to come over?"

"No, please let me talk to Adel."

Adel wanted to come over, too.

I said, "No, just talk to me awhile."

She did, and we ended up with Adel saying, "Well, you'll know tomorrow for sure what's the matter, and maybe they'll have her fixed up in a couple of days."

But I didn't know for sure the next day or the next. On the third day she was operated on for cancer of the stomach. I found that out from Mrs. Swanson, Adel's mom, whose neighbor is a nurse.

My dad only told me Mother was having exploratory surgery. He went to work, went to the hospital, and came home late. I ate sandwiches when I got hungry, and the rest of the time I wandered around the house worrying. Finally, after Mother had been in the hospital a week and a half, Dad said I could go visit with him.

I'd wanted to go so bad, but when I got there I could hardly make my legs carry me down the long white halls. My dad hurried ahead of me and held open the door to Mother's room until I caught up.

She looked so helpless with tubes stuck in her. I blinked my eyes hard as I bent to kiss her pale cheek. Dad stood on the other side of the bed holding her hand. She lay there staring up at him and he stared down at her. I felt left out until she turned her head toward me and asked about school. I said I probably passed even though I missed the finals.

"Why?" she wanted to know.

"I haven't gone."

"You haven't gone!"

"No, I've been worried about you."

"Oh, Didi, I'm going to be fine. It just takes a little while. I'm sorry, though, I won't be able to take you to Mexico this summer."

"That's OK," I mumbled.

A nurse bustled in. "How're you doin'?"

"I could use another shot," Mother told her.

The nurse asked Dad and me to step out for a minute.

"What's the shot for?" I asked him when we were in the hall.

"It eases her pain," he said.

My hand searched through my jacket pocket for a Kleenex.

The nurse came out. "You can go in now."

Dad looked at me. "You can't go in like that."

The nurse patted me on the back. "It takes a little while for her insides to heal. She had a pretty extensive operation, you know."

"I didn't know," I said, and the tears poured out again. My dad stood there until I got it together.

I was smiling when we went back in.

Grandmother says people get sick because they need to or want to. Why would my mother want to have cancer? Didn't she care about me?

That night I lay in bed worrying until I fell asleep and had the dream. It wasn't really a dream. Just a scene. Like a snapshot being flashed in front of me and then yanked away.

I wasn't in the dream, but I saw a girl in a yellow sweater standing next to a teacher's desk, arguing with the teacher. Students were stashed around the room, sitting at desks or tables. A girl with bushy black hair had her face down on the desk, sleeping. Two boys were playing chess at a table, and two other boys were watching the game. There were books on the shelves like in a regular classroom, but the kids acted different, and the teacher didn't get mad at the girl who was arguing with him.

I woke up thinking what a weird scene.

Three

Last summer went by fast like summer always does. It rained and then the north wind blew and the sun came out. It was hot for two days and then the south wind blew and it rained again. Mother came home from the hospital and Grandmother drove up from San Francisco to take care of her. In September I started high school at Alderwood and Dad got a housekeeper in to help. The housekeeper's name was Monica Smith, but she told us her name was Monique. I believed that until I answered the phone and they asked for Monica.

At first Mother was cheerful about her sickness. She even joked when she tried on the wig Grandmother bought her to cover her bald head. I must have looked sad because Mother hugged me and told me her hair would grow back after the chemotherapy was finished.

The chemotherapy made her sick to her stomach, and I played cards with her, trying to make her forget. Sometimes in the middle of the game she'd cover her mouth with her hands. I'd pick up her cards and hold them for her until the nausea passed.

One day, after the card-playing was old and Mother was resting, Grandmother and I had tea alone in the living room. To make conversation, I told her about the school-room dream.

"Were you in the dream?" Grandmother asked me.

"No. Well, I think I was there, watching."

She tilted her head as if she wanted to be certain of every word. "Now, what exactly did you see?"

"I saw a girl telling a teacher off. There were a couple of boys at a table playing chess. They were wearing jeans and T-shirts with something printed on the front. I don't remember what it was, but it was in color. A girl was at another desk sleeping. The whole thing was just one flash."

Grandmother nodded. "It's precognitive."

"What's precognitive?"

"When you drop the illusion of time and find yourself in a probable future." Grandmother picked up her cup and sipped the tea.

I was uneasy, so I talked fast to make myself feel better. "Well, in my high school none of the classrooms are that old and messy. And the kids don't act like that. Anyway, it couldn't be precognitive because it didn't happen."

"Yet," Grandmother said. "If you don't like the picture, you'd better see that it doesn't."

I felt chills go up my arms. "Right now I'd better see how Mother is."

Mother was sitting up in bed feeling under her legs. There was a stricken look on her face.

"Mama!" I said. "What's the matter?"

She stared at me like she didn't see me.

I went closer to the bed. "Mother, what's the matter?"

She didn't answer.

Grandmother sat on the bed and took her by the shoulders. "Anne, what is it?"

Mother's face crumpled. "I've got a lump," she whispered.

"Let me see."

Mother pulled away from Grandmother and looked down at her own hand picking at the quilt. "I already know what it is. The cancer's spreading."

"How do you know?"

"I can feel it in me."

"Anne"—Grandmother's voice was stern—"if that's what you believe, that's what will happen. If not now, later."

I stood up. "That's mean. She's sick."

Grandmother turned around. "Go out and play," she ordered.

"What!!?"

"I mean . . ." She looked flustered. "Go find something to do. You might get dinner for a change."

"I thought Dad hired Monica for that."

Grandmother waved her hand at me. "Go play your records, then. Get out of here."

"She's my mother!" I stamped out of there and up to my room. I was so mad I couldn't do anything but pace from one wall to the other. That old lady had a lot of guts. I kicked over the wastebasket. It was my house, not hers. She wasn't even my mother's grandmother. I kicked the basket again.

When I came down for dinner, Grandmother and Dad were eating in Mother's bedroom. Monica had her brat Cindy with her and they were eating in the kitchen. I dished myself up a plate of food and took it to the living room. I was halfway done when Grandmother came out with Mother's tray.

She looked surprised to see me. "Didi, why are you out here? Why don't you come in with us?"

"I thought I wasn't allowed in there."

"Oh, Didi." Grandmother pursed her lips together. "This isn't the time for that."

"For what?" I asked.

"For thinking about yourself."

Piss on her. I picked up my plate of food, dumped it in the kitchen, and split for Adel's. She and I walked down to Edmonds and stood around Pay 'n Save, twirling the displays of eyeshadow. When I got home, the house was quiet.

In the morning, I stood at the front door in my night-gown, watching Dad put Mother in the car to take her to the hospital for more tests. " 'Bye," I called. "Good luck." She didn't even wave.

Grandmother came into the kitchen while I was eating breakfast. I ignored her. She made herself a cup of tea and sat beside me. I gulped down the last of my grape juice.

"I'm sorry about yesterday," she said. "I was so intent on trying to keep your mother from giving up, I wasn't really paying attention to you."

"I know," I said coldly.

"Didi, I realize she is your mother. . . ."

"Good for you," I said, and left for school.

I hurried down the hall before first period, avoiding my friends. When someone hollered, "Hey, Didi," I went the other way. I took my English book out of my locker, then shoved it back in. Subordinate clauses made me sick. I closed my locker door, hesitated, opened it up again, got my jacket out, and booked.

The salesgirls are never mean at Nordstrom's. Mine stood at the dressing-room door holding my pile of rejects. I tried on mostly pants and sweaters.

"That looks good," the salesgirl said about a navy sweater I had on. "It shows off your red hair."

"Mmmm." I yanked it over my head, plunked it on the reject pile, and reached for some pants.

I got home about three. On the way through the kitchen, Monica told me the school had called. "Where were you this afternoon?" she asked.

"Around," I told her, tasting her lumpy tapioca pudding.

"That's for dessert." She snatched the bowl out from under my spoon. "I'll have to tell your grandmother about the school."

"You do that. She needs something else to worry about." I threw the spoon in the sink.

At dinner Monica went on and on about the terrible 106-degree fever her daughter Cindy had when she was four years old.

"Is that the reason Cindy got held back in school?" I asked her.

Monica stopped dead. "Oh, no. Oh, no. She just needed an extra year in kindergarten to mature."

"Couldn't that be caused by her brain cells being killed off by the fever?"

"No, no. Her brain cells weren't damaged. A high fever isn't unusual for a small child."

"Ohh! The way you were telling it, it sounded like it was unusual."

"Deirdre, if you're finished with your dinner, why don't you serve the dessert?" Grandmother asked me.

I didn't serve myself any pudding. Grandmother took

one bite and decided she was full. Monica gobbled down the whole thing. Actually, Monica was free to go home as soon as she had dinner on, but she stayed and ate. She didn't stay for the dishes, though. I did those.

The rest of the evening dragged on. Grandmother didn't know anything about what was going on at the hospital. Nothing good was on TV. I climbed the stairs to my room and sat at my desk flipping through my French books. About eleven o'clock there was the sound of a car turning in. I raced downstairs. It was Dad, alone. Mother had to stay behind for more tests and treatments.

In the next few weeks I went to classes once in a while. Mostly to French and Spanish because I wanted to hang on to those. If you're absent from a class more than ten days, you have to drop it, for whatever sense that makes. My friends called, trying to cheer me up. Adel tried to coax me to go to parties. I didn't feel like parties.

It was on a Sunday that Dad asked me if I wanted to ride to the hospital with him. As he drove through the traffic, I glanced at his profile. His face had grown hollow below his cheekbones, and his sagging skin pouched under his jaw. Mother used to call him her silent, handsome man. He wasn't handsome anymore.

In her hospital bed Mother looked even smaller and thinner than I remembered. The nurse gently touched her shoulder. "Mrs. Neil," she whispered. "Mrs. Neil, your family's here to visit you."

Mother slowly opened her eyes. She didn't smile when

she saw Dad and me. Just shifted her head a little on the pillow and fell back asleep.

I put the vine maple I'd brought into a vase and filled the vase with water from the sink in the little hospital bathroom. Dad said he thought he'd go down to the lobby and see if he could find some magazines.

I stayed in the room waiting for Mother to wake up, leaning over her each time she stirred. It wasn't just that I wanted to talk to her. I was worried, too. What if she didn't get well?

When Dad came back, he handed me a copy of *Omni* and settled in a chair with *Newsweek*. It must have been an hour before Mother opened her eyes. "Hi, you're awake," I said. "How do you like the vine maple?"

"It's lovely," she said.

"I remembered how you walked in the woods in the fall, so I brought some here for you. I got the branches from the empty lot behind our house like you used to do. Remember?"

She gave me a weak, sweet smile. Dad rose from his chair and took one of her hands. I took the other. We stayed until she drifted off again.

Monica had made soup for dinner. I watched her and Dad and Grandmother dip in their spoons. "Is Mother going to get well?" There it was. Silence all around. If this had been TV, I think all three of them would have spit into their bowls.

Monica put on her sanctimonious look. "Your mother's

gone through a lot. You can't expect her to recover immediately."

"What do you know about it?" I asked her. "Who talks to you?"

"Didi!" my dad said. "That isn't how you treat a guest."

I wanted to say, "I thought she was the hired help," but I decided I better not.

We finished Monica's watery soup. More tapioca pudding. Grandmother didn't bother with it. She buttered herself another roll. I did, too.

The empty, scary feeling came. The kind you get when you first try the diving board. I took a big breath and looked straight at Grandmother. "Is Mother going to die?"

"If that's what she wants to do," Grandmother said.

My dad folded his napkin and rose from the table. "I don't think this is the time for your philosophy, please." He left the room.

I went upstairs to hold Tender Love and cry.

Four

That Monday morning, my mood and the weather were the same, down and damp. I get impatient with the endless gray skies of the Pacific Northwest and feel a desperation for sunshine banging inside me, but sunshine couldn't have helped. I made it off the bus, to the locker, and almost through first period. Right in the middle of the third paragraph of a five-paragraph essay, I got up and walked out of class.

I wove my way through the Camaros and VWs in the student parking lot, hoping to escape the beady eye of Nellie, the narc lady. I made it to the side gate where Crazy Cutler, the VP, popped up from behind a van and hollered, "Wait there just a minute!"

Now Crazy's a big joke, and it's one thing to put him on, but it's another thing to have him usher you through the halls to his office. I tried to walk casually—burning face casual. He sat me down and tilted his desk chair back to the wall. "Early-morning pot party going on down the street?"

I gave him a disgusted stare that had him swing his chair down with a thump and reach for his phone. "Bring me the attendance record for Deirdre Neil, please."

I sat there while he thumbed through my record, mumbling, "Mmmm, hmmm, mmmm, hmmm." He tilted his chair back again, holding the computer printout in his hand. "You haven't been attending regularly, have you?"

"No," I answered.

"Do you have some problem with high school?"

"No."

"Get along with the other kids?"

"Yes."

"Do you understand that you must attend each class eighty hours to get credit? And that means if you're absent more than ten times in a class, you're in a no-credit situation?"

"Yes."

"Yes?"

"Yes, I understand," I said.

"Well, your brain doesn't seem to be controlling your behavior very well, then, does it? You have a boyfriend out of school?"

"No," I said through my teeth.

He sat looking at me for several minutes. "This is the first time you've been caught going off campus, isn't it?"

I nodded.

"And let me give you some advice, young lady. It better be the last time."

I got out of there and headed toward the rest room. Some girl was in one of the stalls, smoking. I took my blusher out of my purse, only I was so nervous I spilled it down my white blouse. While I was dabbing the stain with cold water, the girl came out of the stall and went out the door. I tried to blot my blouse dry with a paper towel.

Nellie, the narc lady, came in. She put her pug nose up in the air, sniffed, pushed the stall door open, peeked in, and then planted her fat self in front of me. "Don't you even bother to flush your cigarette butts down the toilet?"

I kept on scrubbing the front of my blouse. "I don't smoke."

Nellie looked around the walls. "Is there someone else in here? I'm blind?"

I followed Nellie back to Cutler's office.

Students don't explain to a vice principal. The vice principal explains to the students how they are going to have a three-day "vacation" and a suspension notice sent to their parents. I managed to get home to pick the notice out of the mailbox, and the rest of the time I spent wandering around Alderwood Mall. On the fourth day I returned to school and made it to my classes for a week.

We visited Mother on the weekend. When she opened her eyes, Grandmother and Dad talked cheerfully to her. I didn't say much. Mother didn't seem to me to be getting any better, and it made my chest hurt. I tossed around in bed that night, trying to smear away visions of what my life would be like without her. My dad and I hadn't had a fifteen-minute conversation in my fifteen years.

About twelve-thirty I got up. Grandmother was in the living room, reading. She made me a cup of chamomile tea, which she said would help me go to sleep. It didn't. Not until almost morning, and then I slept through my alarm.

When I came into the kitchen, Monica looked surprised. "What are you doing home? The school called, and I said you'd left two hours ago."

"Oh, shit!" I sagged into a kitchen chair.

"I don't want to hear that kind of talk," Monica told me.

"Then don't listen," I told her.

Grandmother came in for coffee.

"You've got to call the high school, Grandmother."

"Why do I 'got to'?" She sat down at the kitchen table.

"Because Monica told the school I'd already left."

Grandmother sipped her coffee. "That's not a big problem. I'll write a note saying you slept in."

"But that won't do it." My voice was getting screechy.

"I'm already in trouble with the vice principal. He'll think I'm lying again."

That interested Monica. She poured herself a cup of coffee and sat next to Grandmother. "Again?" Monica said, like it was any of her business.

I tried to explain. "I didn't lie before. He *thinks* I did. Just because I was in the can when another girl was smoking."

Monica put her elbows on the table and sipped her coffee like Grandmother. "Why didn't you ask him to call in the other girl?"

"No, Monica! You don't understand. She was gone and I was left there with the smoke. Oh, Jee-sus!" It was useless. I started to get up.

Grandmother said sharply, "Didi, what are you doing to yourself? You were simply up in the night and you slept in."

"I'm not doing anything to myself. That Crazy Cutler will do it. He'll kick me out. And you won't help one bit."

Grandmother put down her cup. "I didn't say that, Didi. Before I understood that you had already been in trouble, I said I'd write you a note. Now I'll give Mr. Cutler a call. You eat some breakfast. Monica, fix her some scrambled eggs."

Grandmother went into the living room, and Monica very slowly got up to fix me eggs. Ha. I don't know what Grandmother said on the phone, but when I arrived at

:31

school the secretary told me to see the counselor instead of Cutler.

Kimpton fluffed herself in her seat and asked, "Well, how's everything at home?"

"Fine," I said.

"Your grandmother tells me your mother's ill."

"That's true," I said.

"She's quite ill, isn't she?"

"She has cancer."

"How do you feel about that?"

"How do I feel about what?" I can't help it. As soon as you tell a counselor how you feel, they start pinchin' on your brain like it's a lump of clay.

Kimpton kept her voice down, but I knew she didn't like me much. "I mean, how does your mother being so ill make you feel?"

"Bad," I said.

"And it worries you?"

"Yes."

"What do you worry about?"

"Whether she's going to get well. Whether everything's ever going to be the same again."

"You worry about whether your mother's going to get well?"

I nodded. This was ridiculous.

"What things do you think you can do to help her?"

"I don't know."

"I imagine she needs all her energy to get well, don't

you? And being anxious about your behavior isn't going to help, is it?"

"I don't think she's up to noticing my behavior."

"But your behavior isn't helping other members of the family."

"I guess not."

"Don't you think in a family crisis everybody should do their part?"

And on and on. First they ask you how you feel. Then they tell you how you're supposed to feel—and think. She dismissed me with the parting pinch that she hoped I wouldn't have anything to regret if something happened to my mother.

I didn't even get to the girl's john this time. I went straight for the double doors. Out.

When my unexcused absences piled high enough, Cutler "gave up" on me and dropped me from the school for nonattendance. My dad was shook when he got Cutler's call about the semester suspension. I'd never been a "problem" to him before. Grandmother went on about how people didn't *do* things to me. That I was making my own reality. And was I going to like what I was making?

Dad had to take me to school for my final conference. Things got a little prickly when Dad told Cutler he'd never received the three-day suspension notice or any of my pile of absence slips that had been sent home. I stared out the window while they both stared at me.

"Well," Cutler said finally, "perhaps the best solution is for Deirdre to enroll in the alternative school."

I jerked around to face him. "You mean Cooperation High?" I'd heard about that place. That's where all the dropouts and stoners go.

"Some people like it," Cutler said. "Some students never transfer back to a regular high school. They stay there to graduate."

Big deal. I turned back to the window.

"What's the student body like?" Dad asked Cutler.

"Some of the students have been out of school for a while. Some girls need a place with a nursery for their babies. Some students can't seem to adapt to the regulations we have to impose in a big system, and some just seem to respond better to the informal atmosphere of a small school."

Dad thought all that over for a minute. "Would she be able to return here and graduate with her class?"

"Yes, if she'll attend regularly. The school doesn't have all the subjects we're able to provide, of course. However, the class work is individualized, and she can work as fast as she wants. The credits there count for graduation the same as credits here."

Next, Dad wanted to know how I got enrolled.

I looked at him sideways. "Do I have a choice?"

"No," he snapped.

Enrollment was done through the school district's attendance officer. Cutler called to make an appointment for us. Cooperation took in a new group every two weeks, and he thought I'd be able to start the following Monday.

The attendance officer turned out to be a human being, which was a surprise. While Dad filled out papers, she smiled at me and said she thought I would be happier at Cooperation at this time in my life. She said the teachers at the alternative school understood kids. I guess.

Five

So that's how I ended up in the Coop. When I was on the bus the third day, I wondered why Stacy was in an alternative school. The first time I'd seen Stacy was at a party over Memorial Day. Kids from several high schools in Edmonds were there; they had two kegs and mass weed; and cars were parked three blocks away, so the cops wouldn't get suspicious.

I'd been partying down for a couple of hours, and about one o'clock I wandered out to the deck for some fresh air. I made my way to the railing and was standing in the dark, fingering the buds of a climbing rose, when a rustle at the end of the deck made me turn my head. A boy and girl were silhouetted against the house windows.

He was holding her tight. She had her arms around his shoulders and her lips pressed against the base of his throat. He tilted her chin up and, as he kissed her, his hand trailed from her face down her neck.

The deck flooded with light. Startled, they both stared straight at me. I scrunched my head into my shoulders and faded back through the sliding glass doors to hiss, "Jerk!" at the clod who'd turned on the deck lights.

The second time I saw her was at a kegger, where I asked my friends about her. I found out that she was a sophomore like me, and the boy was Brian, a senior at Fircrest High. It was summer and my mother was sick by then, so I was mostly staying around home, but Adel had come over that night and said Jamison's folks were out and Jamison had a pony keg, come on.

After I'd agreed to go, it turned out that Adel didn't have any money, of course. She told me to tell my grand-mother we needed money for a movie. It doesn't work to lie to my grandmother, so I went to the living room and asked for five dollars to go to a party.

I couldn't lie. I couldn't tell her for a keg. "For refresh-ments," I said.

She raised her eyebrows, but she gave me the five dollars.

At the party, Adel and I found some of our friends sitting around the fireplace, and we joined them. I didn't notice Stacy and Brian there until I got up later to go to the bathroom. Brian, Jamison, and their friend Craddoc were playing a game of pool, and Stacy was watching them.

Stacy's just another brown-eyed girl with long brown hair—unless she's wearing a sweater, which she was that night. I have an all-right figure. But not that all-right.

I didn't see them again until Brian came raging into the rec room, slamming the garden door behind him. "That woman sucks. She really sucks." He went over to the keg, snatched a paper cup off the stack, wrenched the tap open, and slopped beer all over his cup.

Jamison hurried across the floor and put his hand on Brian's shoulder. "Take it easy, man. Take it easy."

Brian whirled his arm into the air, knocking Jamison's hand off his shoulder. "Don't tell me to take it easy!"

Jamison backed up a bit. Brian's big. Craddoc and some of the other guys joined in, and between them they got Brian cooled down and playing another game of pool. Stacy slipped into the room a little later and sat by herself at the end of the davenport. She didn't look at Brian, and he didn't look at her. It went on like that, so after a while I forgot about them and went back to my partying.

I never saw Stacy again until she showed up in Cooperation's office. How she got there might be a mystery, but it wouldn't be too hard to imagine why TJ was in the Coop.

As the bus pulled into the school that third day, I caught reflections of myself in the window. I was wearing a navy blue jacket, jeans, and a light green sweater. With long, curly, carrot-red hair. Aw right. I was ready for TJ.

Only he wasn't there when I got to the orientation room. I picked out a place to sit with empty chairs on both sides.

Stacy took one. I waited. He came in twelve minutes late, pulled out the empty chair, and grinned down at me. Stoned again.

David, our first-period teacher, started in on him. "Why didn't you go to bed last night, TJ?"

"Because I had to work," TJ said.

"Oh? Where do you work?"

"Denny's," TJ said.

"Serving tables?"

"No, washing dishes."

"So that's where you get your money for drugs?"

"Ya," TJ agreed. "What's left after I pay my rent."

I computed that in my head while David passed out our assignment. David knew TJ got stoned. TJ admitted he got stoned. TJ lived alone?

David's assignment was a ditto of capital cities we were to match to countries.

"Romper Room," I said to Stacy.

"Sesame Street," Stacy said to me when Madge, the counselor, came in.

Madge was all hopped up over her hour with us. "First we'll go over your Attitude Scales, and then we'll do something fun."

She passed out the red line graphs of our scores. Stacy's scale was high in alienation from those in authority. Mine was high in academic drive. As soon as I saw that, I turned my profile sheet over and peeked across at TJ's paper. His was way low in manipulation and way low in conformity.

Madge went around the room checking the graphs. She stopped at TJ's seat the longest. His was news?

"You can keep your profile sheets if you want to," Madge said as she walked to the front of the room and pulled down the projector screen.

Larry folded his sheet into a paper airplane and zipped it toward the wastebasket. It landed on the floor near my chair. I looked down and saw his manipulation score was at the top of the graph.

Madge stood in front of the white screen, acting real cute. "Now for the fun part. I'm going to teach all of you to see bioenergetic fields."

"See what?" Larry asked.

"Bioenergetic fields," Madge repeated. "The energy that emanates from each individual."

Oh, auras. I leaned back in my chair.

Madge went on and on about how people in yoga and the occult always said there were colors surrounding bodies, but scientists replied sarcastically, "Sure there are," until the Kirlians in Czechoslovakia discovered a photographic process that reproduced the energy fields of plants, then people. I tipped my chair back farther, and she stopped in the middle of reminding us that artists painted halos around the heads of saints. "You aren't interested in any of this, Deirdre?"

I shrugged.

"Wouldn't you like to see the color of my energy field?" She raised her eyebrows. "Or TJ's?"

Uh, that got me. I slid my chair down and folded my hands. "Yours is blue-green, and it's jumping around now because you're pissed." And that got *her.*

She thought a minute. "I'm not sure pissed is the right word. Disturbed, because I thought I was boring you, and surprised that you could see colors so easily."

"Well, come on," Joe interrupted. "Tell *us* how."

Madge positioned herself in the middle of the white screen. "Just stare here." She pointed to her forehead. "Or here." She pointed six inches above her head. "Let your eyes go out of focus because you have to use the rods in your eyes, not the cones."

The kids all stared at Madge. Beside me, I saw TJ blink. "Don't blink," I told him.

"I see it! I see it!" Larry hollered. "Ohhh, it's gone."

"Don't look right at it," Madge said, "or it will dis-appear. Keep staring at my forehead. You have to use your peripheral vision."

When everybody agreed they at least saw a haze around Madge's head, she called up students to stand in front of the screen. Rita, the girl with the slit shirts, wanted to know what the different colors meant. Madge said they were reflections of the different personalities, and they were all good as long as they were clear. Madge could use a few lessons from my grandmother.

The bell rang before TJ got up front. Just as well. Stacy had a turn, though. That was a surprise for me. A gray cloud sat above Stacy's head.

When we got out of the orientation room for the morning break, TJ fell in right beside me. No weaseling this time. The four of us, Stacy, Larry, TJ, and me, stood around the open court while the guys lit up cigarettes. TJ wanted to know how come I could see auras.

"My grandmother," I told him. "She's really my great-grandmother. I just started calling her Grandmother when I was little because my dad did. She taught me to see auras when I was five. She put a white sheet over the shower rod and held me up in front of the bathroom mirror so I could see my own."

"What else did your grandmother teach you?" TJ asked.

"She tried to teach me how to predict the weather, but you have to meditate to do that and I'd never sit still long enough."

"Big deal around here," Larry said. "Predict rain and you'll be right ninety percent of the time."

"Is she always right?" TJ asked.

"Yep. When I was in grade school, if she told me to wear boots, I'd wear boots. Especially after a camping trip when she stayed dry and the rest of us got wet."

Stacy perked up. "How did she do that?"

"We went up to Canada on a camping trip," I explained. "Me and my mother and father and Grandmother. We were going to stay at this one spot just overnight. Dad looked at the sky and said we wouldn't need tents because there was a north wind and the stars were out. But Grandmother sat under a tree by herself for a while, and then she got up and put together her little pop-up tent. This pissed Dad and he wouldn't help her because he said it was just a waste of time, it wasn't going to rain. She didn't argue with him. She just rolled her sleeping bag out in her tent and crawled in.

"Mother and I woke up in the middle of the night with our hair sopped and our sleeping bags soaked. Dad was stompin' around, throwing our wet gear in the car. Grandmother had a lantern on in her tent, and we could see her dressing, all warm and dry.

"I was scared my dad was going to hit a tree the way he drove the car out of the park. He said to Grandmother, 'I suppose you knew it would rain?' And she said yes, she'd checked the weather before going to bed."

"Shi-it, why didn't she tell him she knew it would rain?" Larry asked.

"He wouldn't have listened to her. He likes to treat her like a crazy lady."

"She sounds spaced," Larry said.

Stacy looked around the court. Most of the kids had gone back to class. "We'd better get going."

As we left for the orientation room, TJ draped his hand on my shoulder. He did the same thing after school, when Larry and he walked Stacy and me partway to the buses. After the boys left us, I said to Stacy, "TJ's eyes are the color of blue crystals."

"Is he ever straight?" Stacy asked. "He could buy a Porsche with the money he spends on dope."

I didn't care. I felt so good I decided to go to Seattle to see Mother. Before I hopped on the Metro, I called Grandmother at the corner gas station to tell her where I'd be.

It was pouring when I got off the bus. I pulled the hood of my jacket over my head and ran for the hospital entrance. I still felt so great I wasn't even put off by the sick smell in Mother's room. I leaned down and kissed her cheek, and it sank under my touch. That brought me down a little, but in a happy voice I asked her how she felt.

She turned her head slowly toward me, as if she were coming up from under water. "You've been at school?"

"Yes, I just got here."

She looked at me a long moment. She seemed to be memorizing my hair, my eyes. "Didi, you're so pretty. . . . Remember when you were three and I took you to a French puppet show and afterwards you pranced around the house, waving your little arms, saying, '*Très bien! Très bien!*' You . . . I . . . ." Her voice drifted off as her eyes lost their focus and the smile faded from her face.

I sat on her bed and held her thin hand, trying not to be scared. "Mother, talk to me some more. Mama, talk to me."

But she wouldn't open her eyes again. After a while I gave up and went home. In the kitchen, Grandmother was making tea and Monica was getting dinner.

"All Mother does is sleep," I complained to Grandmother.

"Sleep is good for her," Monica said in a preachy voice. "She needs strength to get well."

I wasn't talking to *her*. I got myself a Coke and sat down at the table beside Grandmother. "At school today Madge, the counselor, taught the class—"

"Doesn't the counselor have a last name?" Monica asked from the sink.

"I suppose so," I told her. "Anyway, Madge—"

"Does she know you call her Madge?" Monica interrupted again.

"It's an *alternative* school, Monica. We even call the principal *Ruth. Anyway,* we looked at auras in class today, and there was a gray cloud above one girl's head."

Monica stopped peeling carrots. "You looked at *what*?"

"Bioenergetic fields around human beings," I told her.

"What kind of high school subject is that?" Monica demanded.

"Who knows?"

She gave a carrot a swipe, and half of it fell in the sink. "You'd better get yourself back to a regular school."

Grandmother carefully tried the hot tea in her cup. "Is the girl depressed?"

"Maybe," I said. "I wonder what Mother's aura looks like now."

Grandmother didn't answer me.

"Mother acts like she's on a trip of her own."

"She's probably preparing herself for one," Grandmother agreed.

"What does that mean?" I waited. My good mood was gone, and my Coke was getting sticky sweet. "Well?"

Grandmother didn't answer that, either.

I squeezed the Coke can flat. "Sometimes you're so damned mysterious, it pisses me off."

Monica put her wet hands on her hips, dripping water down her dress to the floor. "I suppose that school teaches you to talk nasty, too."

"Of course," I told her. "And you better watch out. You're making clean spots on the floor."

I tossed the Coke can in the garbage. Miserable day.

Six

After school on Friday we were standing in front of the buses when Rita came wingin' by and tapped TJ on the back. "Comin' to my party Saturday night?"

"Sure," TJ said, "we'll all come."

"Pony keg or horse keg?" Larry wanted to know.

"Bring your own," Rita said, and climbed on her bus.

"I can get you some good skunk weed," Larry called after her.

"Skunk weed?" Stacy asked.

"Indica," TJ explained. He put his hand on my shoulder. "You and Stacy come."

"Maybe," I said.

"You can find it easy," Larry said. "She lives in a little yellow house back in the woods next to Fowkes Park."

Stacy and I looked at each other. Rita?

"She has rockin' parties," Larry said.

"I bet," I said.

My bus driver started up the engine. TJ held me back a second. "Be there. I'll come after work."

Saturday morning, Adel called and wanted me to go to a show with her. I told her I couldn't, that I already had plans. I could have asked her along to Rita's party, but . . . I don't know. I was a little self-conscious about the things that were happening to me. And Adel's life was still Spanish 3 and 4 and football games.

I looked up Stacy's number in the phone book. I figured I'd have to do some talking to get her to go. There was a long silence after I brought up the party. Then, "All right, I'll go, but why don't you come over for dinner first and stay all night? It will be easier to come back here together."

I wasn't sure of the logic of that. Especially since I was hoping to be with TJ. However, I picked up that it would be better not to argue the details.

Stacy's mom cooked as well as mine. I could smell the chicken baking as soon as Stacy let me in the door. While we ate, Stacy's dad bragged about all the big civilian jobs he was about to be offered because he'd done purchasing for the navy. Stacy's mom didn't say much. Her eyes are brown like Stacy's, but she has yellow hair which she knots low on the back of her neck. She'd look sort of classy if she'd stand up straight. There's a hump above her shoulder blades, and she slumps into her chest as if she's waiting for a hailstorm. Stacy's dad bossed her around and got mad when he poured gravy on his potatoes and it was cold. Mrs. Reynolds snatched the pitcher off the table and hurried into the kitchen to reheat the gravy.

The whole thing made me nervous, and I was glad when dinner was over and Stacy and I went to her room. She got out her tapes and we listened to them until it was party time.

There were mass people at Rita's. Larry was carrying a cranked-up blaster and held it out for us to see. "All it cost me was five fingers!"

I saw TJ weave through the crowd with a big grin on his face. He put his arm around me and herded us over to the side of the room where he had his bong stashed. We all settled down under a fern with our backs to the dining-room wall and watched the crowd mill.

Rita was wearing black silky pants and a black scoop-neck blouse. She has bushy black hair, anyway, and it was in corkscrew curls all over her head.

Larry bent forward, squinting. "What's with her hair?"

"That's a permanent, man," TJ said. "Industrial strength."

Joe came swinging through the middle of the room with a bottle of 151 hanging from his hand. Somebody grabbed at the bottle to take a swig and the rum spilled on the floor. Rita started yelling to clean it up before it spotted her mother's rug.

A game of "Bizz-Buzz" started up beside us. TJ got us some beers so we could play, too. When he handed Stacy a bottle, she took it uncertainly. "But I don't know how to do this."

Larry leaned in front of Stacy, and held his bottle up to her face with his fingertips around the cap. "You twist this round metal part like so . . ."

She shoved him away. "No, bat's breath, the game."

"It's easy," TJ explained. "You count around the circle, everyone saying a number. Only for five and multiples of five, you say 'Bizz,' and for seven and multiples of seven, you say 'Buzz.' If you mess up on the count, you take a drink of beer. If you forget to say 'Bizz' or 'Buzz,' you take another drink. Got it?"

Stacy nodded and we squirmed around the floor until we were all in the circle. The count began.

"One, two, three, four, Bizz, six, Buzz, eight, nine, Bizz, eleven, twelve, thirteen, Buzz."

"Fifteen," Larry said, and everybody yelled at him. It seemed to me he liked the attention because he couldn't stifle a grin as he took his first swig.

"Sixteen, seventeen, eighteen, nineteen, Bizz, Buzz, twenty-two, twenty-three, twenty-four, Bizz, twenty-six."

"Buzz," Stacy said.

I pushed her. "No, no. Multiples of seven, silly."

Stacy flapped her hands in front of her face. "I thought it was twenty-eight. I thought the next one was twenty-eight."

50:

"Drink your beer," TJ told her, and reached out and pulled me closer to him. Out of the corner of my eye I saw a flash of red through the window above us.

Larry stiffened. "Pigs!" He had that window yanked open and was out of it before I figured out what was going on. TJ pushed Stacy through, jumped out, and pulled me after him.

We split for the trees in back of the house. Kids were pouring out of that place like it was on fire. I was staggering after TJ through strange backyards, and bodies kept zipping by me in the dark. We were about three blocks away before anybody slowed down. TJ let go of my hand and put his arm around my waist as we walked along.

We ran into Larry halfway to Stacy's house. He was clutching his blaster under his jacket, and every time a car came our way he jumped in the bushes. Stacy told him sharply to get it together when he banged into her, but he kept mumblin' about not going back to the training school for no party. He split down an alley before we got to the Reynoldses'.

TJ told Stacy to go in and I'd be in in a minute. He walked me over to the side yard, and we leaned against the fence because it was too damp to sit on the grass. I came about up to TJ's chin. At first his kisses were soft and dry and warm. Then he got into it. And I got into it. I surprised myself. It wasn't any first time, but it was the first time I felt like that.

The warmth melted my bones, and I curved against TJ's

body. His hand was low on my back, holding me tight, and it was lucky, because my knees wanted to give. I didn't want the night ever to stop. But TJ stopped. With his arms wrapped around me, and my head tucked under his chin, he held me until I could feel his breathing slow and his heart slow.

He put his hands on my shoulders and moved me away from him, leaned down, and kissed me gently on the forehead. " 'Night, Didi."

I crept through Stacy's dark living room to the bathroom. As I brushed my teeth, I watched my face in the mirror. My cheeks were rosy and my eyes shiny. I wished TJ could have seen me in the dark.

"Well?" Stacy said when I got into bed.

"Hmmm, he's yummy."

"I hope you're on the pill."

I giggled. It took me a long time to fall asleep, thinking about what *that* would be like. With TJ.

Something woke me up about an hour later. I lay still in the bed until voices from the living room pierced through the bedroom wall.

"I said channel *seven,* not eleven, you stupid bitch."

"I didn't hear you. You were mumbling," Stacy's mother said.

"Don't tell me what I'm doing." His voice was harsh, and I heard a thump and then Mrs. Reynolds cried out.

I sat up and turned on the light. "Stacy, wake up. Your parents are fighting."

Stacy just lay on the bed with her eyes open. She hadn't been sleeping at all.

There was another thump and a scream. I started to shake.

"Stacy, you'd better go out there quick. He's drunk and he'll hurt your mother."

"She gets hurt all the time," Stacy said.

"What?"

"She gets hurt all the time," Stacy repeated.

I sat there shaking, wanting to go home, but the hall led to the living room. I looked at the window and wondered if I could climb out.

"You can climb out and go home if you want," she said in a dead voice.

"Oh, no, that's all right." I turned out the light and pulled the covers back up. I was ashamed to have Stacy know what I was thinking.

Footsteps ran to the bathroom door and the door closed. Then a thudding down the hall and banging on the door. The door opened and Stacy's mother said, "Please, Ken, please, the girls."

The door slammed shut. Rustling sounds. Later, footsteps went back down the hall and there was silence.

Mrs. Reynolds was making pancakes by the time Stacy and I got out of the shower in the morning. Stacy's dad wasn't anywhere around, so I guessed he was sleeping. I tried to peek at Mrs. Reynolds's face when she brought the platter of pancakes to the table, but she kept her head turned away. After we finished breakfast, Stacy said we'd clean up the kitchen.

"No, I haven't got anything else to do. Why don't you girls go to the park? It's a beautiful day out." Mrs. Reynolds ran hot water over the pancake turner in the sink for what I thought was an extra long time.

"OK," Stacy agreed. "Come on, Didi."

As I followed Stacy out of the kitchen, I took a last look at her mother. The whole side of her face was swollen.

There was no one in the park when we got there. A wind came up and blew the clouds over the sun, leaving the place chilly and damp. Stacy and I walked over to the benches by the wading pool and sat down. I kept thinking about her mother's swollen face.

"How come you didn't try to help your mom?"

Stacy twirled the strap on her purse. "It doesn't do any good. He just gets madder."

"How long has she put up with him?"

"He's been gone a lot—in the navy. He was overseas the last two years. Mom and I stayed with her sister Katherine. Mom worked a bit in Katherine's florist shop. It was fun. Just the three of us. Then he retired two and a half months ago."

"Does your mom still work?"

"Only on Fridays . . . and Friday night." She stared out over the park as if she were seeing things I couldn't see. "Any chance I could stay with you next Friday night?"

"Sure," I agreed. Who would want to be in the house alone with that father?

It was too cold in the park. As we walked out, I asked her how come she wasn't going to Fircrest.

"Because I took off for a couple of weeks, and when they brought me back, the school said I'd missed too much and I'd better transfer to Cooperation."

"You ran on account of your dad?"

Stacy nodded.

We were at the edge of the park by then, and I stopped before turning toward my house. "He beats you, too, huh?"

"No," Stacy said. And she hurried off down the street.

Seven

At school Monday, everyone was talking about Rita's party getting busted. Larry went around bragging about how he was the first to spot the cops and how he broke open the window and led us all to safety.

TJ shook his head. "No, no, Larry. You lost it. You jumped in more bushes than Br'er Rabbit."

"No way," Larry said. "I did *not* lose it. I was being careful. If I get busted, my PO'll send me back up. And I ain't going back up."

The PO part was news to me.

On Tuesday, TJ didn't come to school. I saved an empty seat and expected him every minute. Each time the classroom door opened, I turned around. But TJ never came. I asked Larry after first period if he knew where TJ was. He said he didn't know. The day got longer and longer. The assignments were dumb. Orientation is dumb, anyway. Nobody needs to be oriented into a school for *two* weeks.

Madge started making out our class schedules on Wednesday, which was a relief. To keep us busy, she had us write partial autobiographies. A slice of life, she called it. I wrote about the time my dog followed me to kindergarten.

I was on the part where I was standing on the parking strip staring at the dog catcher as he put a noose around my dog's neck, when Madge called me up. She had my withdrawal form from Alderwood and a blank class schedule on her desk. I sat down in front of her.

"We can put you in English ten, U.S. history, and PE," she said, writing those subjects down.

I nodded.

"And then how about an art and home ec class?"

"Wait a minute! I was taking geometry, Spanish three, and French three."

She smiled brightly. "We only go till one o'clock, so you'll have five classes here instead of six. And we only teach general math."

"OK, but what about my Spanish and French?"

"We don't have any foreign languages."

"What!"

"That's right. There are ten teachers for two hundred

and fifty students. If one teaches home ec and another PE and another biology and another—"

"Wait a minute," I interrupted. "That means I can't get in four years of foreign language and I'll have to take geometry and French and Spanish three and four all over."

"You're just a sophomore," she said.

"Just a sophomore! I have my junior and senior years all planned. And you're telling me I'll have to take everything over next year? What's the point of even going here?"

She paused to tell Joe and Larry to get to work. "The school's on a continuous-progress program, Didi. You're a smart girl, and if you work hard you can pick up a couple of extra credits in English and social studies in no time."

"But I'll still be behind in foreign language and math."

"Well, that's the way it goes. Do you want me to put down art and home ec or would you rather have typing?"

"Put down anything you want," I said, getting up. "This school obviously sucks."

I sat on the log in front of the art room going over my whole shitty life, and where was TJ, anyway? Stacy came down the walk and sat next to me on the log. At first I wanted to tell her to go back to class, but after a few minutes there was a comfort in her sitting quietly beside me.

The bell rang, and Simon, the art teacher, followed a bunch of kids out of his art room. "Can I walk you girls to class?" he asked us.

He started to walk between us, taking both our arms,

but Stacy slipped to the other side of me. I noticed she kept her distance from men.

"How do you like it here, so far?" Simon wanted to know.

"I hate it," I said.

Simon bumped his elbow against me. "What do you mean, you hate it? What's to hate? Next week the whole school's walking down to Edmonds to see *The Seven Samurai*. You can't say you'll hate that."

"I've already seen *The Seven Samurai*," I said.

"Then you know how good it's going to be. For Halloween we turned the art unit into a haunted house and invited special-ed children. The art students painted the little kids up like punks. They had a great time."

"What's that got to do with school?" I asked.

Simon looked down at me. "Being a kind human being isn't important?"

I looked right back at him. "No school was ever kind to me."

"Me either," Stacy mumbled.

That didn't faze Simon a bit. "You two made the best folder designs in orientation. You'll be great in this place."

Madge came out of the orientation room just as we got to the door. She took a quick glance at me before saying hi. I wondered if she had scheduled me into art, but I was too proud to ask.

At the end of the day, I couldn't help asking Larry if he

thought TJ was sick. He grinned, showing his rabbity teeth.
"He probably had a woman over last night and they slept
in. You know TJ."

I couldn't figure out if he was kidding or not. I sat on
the bus going home wishing I knew where TJ's house was.
House? Room? I should have asked Larry.

The two Oriental boys in the Coop were sitting in the
seat in front of me chattering away. It would be fun to
learn Chinese. I wondered if maybe I could get them to
teach me a little bit. . . . I flashed on tutors. If I had a
tutor, I could keep up with my French and Spanish. Or at
least Spanish. I shifted in my seat, getting into the idea. If
I could get Mother awake and listening . . . I hopped
off the bus at the next stop and caught the Metro to
Seattle.

Twenty minutes of shaking her shoulder. Not a stir.
"Mama," I coaxed, "please try to wake up. I need to talk
to you. You have to help me make some plans."

Frustration welled in me as I watched her closed lids.
Not a flutter. I threw up my hands helplessly, paced the
floor, sat on the hard, plastic hospital chair, paced the
floor.

Grandmother walked into the room, and I turned on
her. "You're always telling me that I make my own reality.
How can I do it when she won't wake up?" I pointed to
Mother, lying on her side, curled into an S shape like a
baby.

Grandmother put the vase of flowers she was carrying

onto the windowsill before she stared around Mother's head, which lay like a stone on the white pillow. "I think if you have some things to say to her . . ."

"I do. I've been trying."

"No," Grandmother said. "I mean, if you have something you want to say as a daughter to her mother."

A vise of fear closed over my chest, preventing the meaning of her words from circulating in my brain. "But she's sleeping."

"She can hear you. I'll go outside while you talk to her." Grandmother left the room.

I stood paralyzed a moment before walking over to the bed and sitting on the edge to look down at my mother. If only she'd open her eyes again, and if I could see them, green like mine, it would be easy to talk to her, tell her I loved her. But she wasn't going to open her eyes.

Tears poured down my face, and I took two shuddering breaths before I could begin. "Mama," I whispered, "I'm sorry I wasn't a better daughter for you. I'm sorry I yelled at you when my dress wasn't finished for Adel's party. After you worked most of the night on it. I'm selfish. I'm sorry I was so selfish.

"I'm sorry I didn't sit with you more while you were sick. I'm sorry I didn't stay home with you more when you were well. Maybe if you'd had more company and weren't alone so much . . ." I leaned and patted her head. "I love you, Mama, I really love you. Even if I wasn't a good daughter to you, I love you."

I wiped my arm across my eyes. " 'Bye, Mama," and I stumbled out of there.

Grandmother was outside the door, waiting for me. She took me in her arms and held me.

"I should have been more company. Then maybe she'd have been happy."

Grandmother gently moved me back from her. "You couldn't have made her happy, Didi. That's something she had to learn to do herself."

"I could have helped."

"You did help. You were the joy in her life."

I shook my head. "I should have done more."

"No." Grandmother brushed the hair from my forehead. "It wouldn't have made any difference. She didn't have the will to go through the changes she needed to make."

I thought about that. Maybe it was true. She was still a lovely mother.

It was a long time before I fell asleep that night. And not long after I did, I was awake again. I felt Mother in my room. It was dark and I couldn't see clearly to the end of the bed, but she was there. Her soft presence soothed me until I slipped back to sleep.

The next time I awoke, it was to the ringing of the telephone. Grandmother's calm voice. My father's trembling voice. I met them at the bottom of the stairs and knew by his white face. Grandmother guided us into the living room. The sound of a man's grief is different from a woman's. A man's sobs are harsh and choked.

Eight

Stacy came in the afternoon and rocked quietly in my rocker while I lay on my bed. "When's the funeral?" she asked.

"Tomorrow evening," I said, not lifting my arm away from my face. "We have to wait for Rose, my dad's mother, to get here. And my other grandparents. It's just going to be a little family memorial in the church chapel."

The rocking went on. Tomorrow was Friday night, but I had no memory for plans with Stacy. My mind held only pain. Stacy touched my hand softly and went away.

TJ came Friday afternoon and put his arm around my shoulders as I sat in the living room, dressed up, waiting to make the trip to the airport to get Rose. "Where've you been?" I asked.

"Working two shifts. The cook was drunk." He tried to make me smile. "Cooking is easier on your hands than washing dishes."

At the service I cried out once when the minister said, Anne Neil. During the rest of his eulogy, I sank my teeth into my fingers to keep from making another sound. Mother's parents huddled together in the end pew. Grandpa was murmuring, "Why couldn't it have been me? Why couldn't it have been me?" His trembling voice made my chest quiver with choked sobs.

TJ came again Sunday. He took me for a walk along Edmonds Beach and told me what it was like when he was nine years old and his mother died. "That must have been rough," I said.

He held my hand tight. "It's rough anytime, huh, Didi?"

I nodded, concentrating on the sand beneath our shoes. I couldn't have chanced saying how bad it hurt. We chose one of the logs lining the edge of Puget Sound and sat down to watch the big white ferry from Kingston come into dock. "Is your dad gone, too?" I asked.

TJ leaned over, picked out a small, flat rock, and zipped it across the water. "No, he's around."

"You don't like him?"

"Sure, he's a good guy. He and I batched together for five years until he met Clarise and she and her two kids moved in. That was OK until she and my dad got married. After that, Clarise took over and I moved out."

I turned my jacket collar up. The November cold was

seeping down my neck. TJ took my hand and pulled me
to my feet. As we walked back, I asked, "What is your
dad like, anyway?"

"He's a laid-back, easygoing guy. He liked to go salmon
fishing and drink beer before he met Clarise. I guess he
thought getting married again would be like being married
to my mom."

On my porch, TJ tipped up my chin and kissed me good-
bye and went off to wash dishes at Denny's.

Grandmother and Rose were having glasses of white
wine in the living room. As I came downstairs from putting
my jacket away, I heard Rose say, "What a wasted life
Anne had. I can't think of anything stupider than trying
to make a career out of being Raymond's wife. He's never
been a people person."

She changed the subject when I walked in. "Mother,
don't let me forget to call Walter Brown before I leave. I
want these eyelids tucked up."

Grandmother squinted at her. "They look fine to me."

"When I get tired, they don't. It will be a year before I
can get an appointment. They'll be drooping worse by
then." She sipped her wine and looked Grandmother over.
"You should do something about those wattles."

Grandmother pulled on the loose flesh under her chin.
I hadn't really noticed it before. She looks good to me, for
seventy-six years old, even if her daughter is a grandma.

I don't call Rose Grandma. She isn't the type. She's fifty-
six, has a small, wiry body and short, curly red hair. *And*

she's part of an aerial act. In grade school I bragged about her. I had to cut that out in junior high because, when I'd say my grandma was in the circus, some smart ass would always ask, "What is she? The bearded lady?"

When Dad came home, Rose got up and gave him a big hug. He stood there stiffly, leaning back like he does. She might as well have hugged a wooden plank. "Well, how's the pharmacy business on Sunday?" she asked him.

"Fine," Dad said. "I think twenty percent of the women in this suburb are on Valium."

"Those are the ones who have no life of their own," Rose said.

Dad poured himself some wine. "Then I guess you'll never need it."

"I don't intend to," she snapped.

That ended that discussion, and they talked about nothing much until Monica called us for dinner.

Rose stirred the food around on her plate as she had last night. "Good Lord," she said after Monica left the table to get dessert, "we get better food than this at a concession stand."

I hung around downstairs until everyone had gone to bed, avoiding as long as possible the sad memories that came in the night.

Monday I returned to school and was held in orientation for two more days. TJ and Larry were there, too, making up time. I looked all around for Stacy during the morning break. Finally I found her smoking out with Larry in the back of the basketball court. Their eyes were lit up like headlights on high beam. They stunk, too. Luckily for Larry, the next class was Ellen's hour and she didn't notice. I guess they don't teach about stoners in church.

Dianna, the secretary, had been more places than church, though. The next day, when we all trooped into the office before lunch to get field trip passes, she said, "What's that smell? What *is* that smell?"

And Larry said, quick like a fox, "Oh, the bus driver hit a skunk on the way to school."

"That's too bad," Dianna said, and began handing out our passes for the movie on Friday. She stopped at Larry. "Just a darn minute. Let me smell your hands."

"Smell Joe's first. I gotta go to the can." Larry split down the hall to the lavatories.

Dianna leaned over the counter and yelled, "Larry, you get back here!" But he was gone.

Joe held out his hands.

She sniffed. "You're OK." She gave Joe a pass.

I held out my hands. This was unreal. She smelled them and gave me a pass.

"I need two," I said. "One for Stacy back there."

She gave me two. I grabbed the passes and pushed Stacy down the hall. We met Larry coming out of the boys' john. His stink was gone.

"That was stupid," I told Stacy in the girls' room. "Where'll you go if you get kicked out of here?"

Tuesday I finished my folder, and Wednesday I was out

of orientation. TJ had to stay in another day. I didn't have art with Stacy. I had typing instead. Stacy and I were together in home ec and David's social studies class, though.

David gave us a choice of stuff to do. Read books and report to him, answer sets of his questions, or read a text and answer questions at the end of the chapters. We chose reading books. I took *Black Elk Speaks,* because I'd seen my grandmother reading it, and Stacy took *The Spirit of St. Louis.* "Beats making a U.S. history credit in a regular high school," I said.

Stacy agreed.

When I got tired of reading, I watched Rita from across the room. She was tossing her black hair back and forth and tapping her foot against the leg of the table. I bet she was on speed.

She beat Stacy and me out the door for the morning break. TJ and Larry were already in the yard lighting up. As soon as Larry saw Stacy he raised his eyebrows. She nodded and they took off for the back of the basketball court.

Stacy got gonzoed with Larry again on Friday. I was disgusted. "Stacy, you're acting just like all the rest of the stoners in the Coop," I told her on the way back from the movie.

"So?" Stacy said. "What's the difference between us and them?"

"They're a bunch of losers," I said.

"We're winnin'?" Stacy asked.

I Never Asked You to Understand Me

I walked along, pulling leaves off the rhododendron bushes that lined the yards. Grandmother says you make your own reality. How do you do it? Wave a wand that brings your mother back? Wave another wand that takes Stacy's dad away?

"Can I come over after dinner and stay with you?" Stacy asked suddenly.

I looked at her, surprised. "Uh . . . sure," I said, "if you want to."

On my way home, the sounds of wailing reached me even before I got to my back door. I peeked through the kitchen window to see what was going on inside. There was Cindy standing in front of Monica, flailing her arms and yowling.

It didn't look like Monica had hit her because Monica's face was screwed up with concern and she seemed to be trying to quiet Cindy. It wasn't doing any good. Cindy's arms waved more wildly, and her cries grew louder. Monica reached out and drew her close, wiping her eyes with a dish towel. Cindy's yowling petered down to sniffles as Monica stroked her forehead and cooed to her.

Maybe the kids at school had teased Cindy. Maybe she'd flunked a test. No, she was too upset for a test. The kids must tease her. Monica handed Cindy the dish towel to blow her nose and took a package of Oreos out of the cupboard, which was dumb. Cindy didn't need more calories.

Cindy smiled up at her mother as she crunched the cookies in her mouth. Monica smiled fondly back at her. Monica was a jerk, but she loved her ugly duckling. A sickish empty feeling spread through my insides. I hurried around to the front door and up to my room, where I stood at the window looking down at the irises Mother had tended so carefully.

Dead brown leaves curled around the weathered plants. Mother would have had their green swords cut in half and the ground around them neatly mounded with bark. It was the least I could do. I found her garden clippers and gloves in a willow basket on a shelf in the garage, and as I worked around her beloved irises, tears dropped into the dirt.

When Monica yelled that dinner was ready, I got up slowly from the ground. Grandmother and Rose were shopping in Seattle. Dad was at his pharmacy. Alone on the dining-room table sat greasy meat loaf and half-cooked potatoes. I finished the package of Oreos in the kitchen.

I was still down and hungry when Stacy came over. Instead of talking to her, I lay on my bed reading. She put her toothbrush in the bathroom and combed her hair and rocked in my rocker, leafing through some old *Rolling Stone*s. Her quietness finally seeped into me, and I closed my book.

She looked up. "Do you wish I hadn't come over, Didi?"

"Oh, no," I said. "I'm just bummed out because the food the housekeeper cooks is unfit to eat."

She turned a page. "That's too bad."

She turned another page and let out a shaky sigh. I felt ashamed. She'd been nice to me. I hoped she wouldn't cry.

I Never Asked You to Understand Me

Her brown eyes glistened, her face was white, and a tinge of yellow came around her mouth. I felt so mean.

I got up and squeezed into the rocker with her and hugged her. "Don't cry, Stacy. You can stay here every night that your mom works."

She shook her head.

"Come on, Stace. It's no big deal."

She stared at me intently. "You sure you don't mind?"

I wiped her wet cheek with a sleeve of my nightgown. "I'm sure," I said. "Come on. Let's crash."

I took a good look at her when she stripped off her clothes to put on her pajamas. No bruises. I had been wondering why she ran away, so I asked her after we piled into bed.

"Because of my dad," she said.

"Because he beats your mother?"

"No."

"Well, why then?"

She didn't answer. She's not the easiest person to get talking. I was used to Adel, whom you can't shut up.

"What did he do?"

"He got drunk."

"And?"

"He drank a half rack of beer."

"And?"

"Well, he got drunk."

"You said that."

"I know." She started again. "He was getting drunk.

And saying things like how I'd grown up since he'd been gone and he bet the boys noticed me and did a boy ever bother me. I said I supposed so and he wanted to know exactly what the boy did. He was leaning over my chair, and his eyes were all bloodshot, and he was making me tell him exactly what the boy tried to do. I felt creepy so I finished my Coke, and I took the can into the kitchen and then walked back into the living room and said good night and split for my bedroom. He yelled that he wasn't finished talking to me, but I pretended I didn't hear him and started getting undressed—"

The phone was ringing downstairs. I hopped out of bed. "Just a sec, Stacy. I'll be right back."

It was Adel. Another party. I told Adel no thanks, I'd catch her later. How soon, Adel wanted to know. Soon, I said. When I got back in the bedroom, Stacy was lying flat on her back, staring up at the ceiling.

"It was only Adel." I put out the light and climbed in beside her. "Now what was this about your dad?"

"Nothing. He's just a shit."

"I know that, but what did he do after you went to your room?" I waited. "What, Stacy?"

"Let's go to sleep." There was a hard edge to Stacy's voice that ended my questions.

Nine

"I don't want to be a drag," I told TJ on the phone Saturday, "but I'm not up for much."

"No problem," he said. "Let's go to the Laserium at the Seattle Center by ourselves."

We were early, so we walked around the water fountains, stared at the old space capsule hanging from the cement wall, and shivered in the icy weather until the door opened. The Laserium is a round room with a carpeted floor on one half circle and swivel-back chairs on the other half. A huge white dome covers the area.

TJ said the best place was in the middle-front, lying on your back. "Isn't that too close to the speakers?" I asked, eyeing the orange panels mounted on the wall a few feet away from us.

"Once the show starts, you'll never notice." He stretched out on the carpet. I lay down beside him.

While the crowd was settling down, synthesizer music blasted over us like galloping horses. Three boys found spots next to me. I wiggled closer to TJ. The music faded, and the laser operator announced that this evening we would have "The Best of Zepplin."

"Aw right!" TJ said.

"You see something you like, that just happens to make you happy, let me know," the operator advised us.

The theater darkened, swirls of color poured down from the ceiling, pulsing with the beat of the music. The laser lights burst into skyrocket bits of red, yellow, and blue, transformed into a zeppelin, and flowed into stairways to heaven. TJ was right. I was conscious only of the sound and images fusing into a total sensation, and after each piece ended and the crowd yelled, "Louder!" I yelled, too.

When the lights formed the words "Thank You," moans went up. "More, more! Encore!" we pleaded.

"You want another one?" the operator asked. "I didn't know if you could handle it. Well, wait a minute until I get it ready."

We yelled.

"Be patient," he said. "Just twenty more minutes."

We roared.

"OK," the operator said, "here we go." And the lights came down in waves and the music flowed through us again. Beside me, TJ sang, his voice threading through the song, shifting with the spinning patterns.

"You should be a singer," I said to him as we left the Laserium.

"I sing with Joe's band," he said.

"Joe has a band?"

"He's trying out one. Come to the rehearsal next Friday?"

"OK, but what are you doing on Thursday?" I asked.

"Probably treating myself to Denny's deluxe turkey sandwich," he said. "It's my birthday on Thanksgiving. Maybe I'll have two turkey sandwiches."

"How old will you be?"

"Seventeen."

I took hold of his arm. "Have Thanksgiving with us. I'll put a candle on the pumpkin pie."

"I'm working that night."

"Come over at three, then. We'll eat by four. Only come *straight*, OK?"

TJ raised an eyebrow. I probably shouldn't have said that. We threaded our way through the trees in the Center and walked across the grass to the street. "What I don't understand," I said, "is how your stepmother just took over."

"Gradually," TJ answered. "First she wanted the house

painted and a new rug, and my dog kept outside. Then shrubs around the house and new grass, and one day I came home and my dog was gone.

"She said my bedroom was the biggest and I should give it to her boys because they needed a place to play. I took the little room and put a lock on the door to keep her kids out, but the day I forgot to shut my room, she went in and found some weed. She got hysterical and screamed that I'd make junkies out of her children. I packed up."

"What about your dad?" I wondered. "Didn't he care if you left?"

"Sure, he came in while I was packing and said Clarise would calm down, just keep the drugs out of the house. But she'd already gotten on my case really bad after I got suspended for smoking. I tried to explain to her that I couldn't get through third period without going crazy, so she bought me some nicotine gum."

"Did it work?"

"Hell, no. It gave me a big lump in my chest and felt like a burrito was stuck in my throat. When I got suspended again, she decided I was a bad example for her kids. She was out to get rid of me just like she had my dog."

"That's mean," I said.

"That's life." He shrugged.

Before dinner the next day I told Grandmother I had invited TJ for Thanksgiving and asked her if we could give Monica the day off. Grandmother said she thought that would be nice for Monica. Monica didn't think so.

"I already ordered the turkey!" she complained.

"That's fine. Didi and I can cook it," Grandmother said calmly. "You deserve the holiday off."

Monica turned and pointed the pancake turner at me. "How come your boyfriend isn't eating at his own house?"

"Because he doesn't get along with his stepmother."

She shoved the pancake turner under the hamburger patties and slapped them on a platter. She was pretty quiet during dinner, but I noticed she gave Dad the biggest piece of cake, which was eatable because it was store bought. During dessert she said to no one in particular, "With this sudden change of plans, I just don't know what Cindy and I will do on Thanksgiving."

Her whiny voice caught Dad's attention. "Why don't you eat with us?"

Monica swirled her spoon in her coffee cup. "Didi and her grandmother want to make dinner themselves—for Didi's boyfriend."

"Well, you can come, too. Can't you?"

"If you're sure you all don't mind. Cindy and I make such a little family."

Monica always goes limp and helpless around Dad, and he bites every time. I thought fast. We could give Monica the fruit salad to make. She couldn't wreck that.

Thanksgiving morning I heard Grandmother get up early. I hurried and dressed and ran into her in the bathroom. She was standing in front of the mirror stretching her neck skin up under each ear.

"You look fine the way you are, Grandmother," I told her.

"I *hate* being old," she said, and marched out of the bathroom.

Rose set the table with Mother's flowered porcelain plates, Grandmother made the dressing and prepared the turkey for the oven, and I candied sweet potatoes and mixed the batter for the pies. Unfortunately, my idea for Monica to do the fruit salad wasn't fail-safe.

Grandmother caught her just before she dumped a bag of miniature marshmallows into the bowl. "I don't think those will be necessary. We have enough fresh fruit."

Monica put her hands on her fat hips. "I think they make the salad look pretty."

"Perhaps," Grandmother said, "but we won't use them this time."

Monica jammed the marshmallows back in the cupboard. It was a bit uncomfortable in the kitchen, so I was glad when Stacy called. Her dad was out of town interviewing for a job, and she and her mother were having dinner at her aunt Katherine's apartment. I bet her mother was making the pies. Stacy said she was.

TJ arrived at three-thirty. I took one good look at him when he got inside the doorway. "You might have come straight."

"Who'll know?" He slipped off his jacket and gave it to me.

"Grandmother will know. How much did that weed cost, anyway?"

TJ reached for his jacket. "Maybe I'd better get a turkey sandwich at Denny's."

"No, TJ. I'm sorry."

I took him into the living room and introduced him to Grandmother, Rose, and Dad. From the way Rose looked over TJ, I could see she appreciated his body. Some grandma.

TJ was very polite at the dinner table. He complimented Grandmother on the turkey and dressing and asked who made the excellent salad.

"I did," Monica said, pleased.

Rose turned to me. "How's your Spanish coming?"

"It isn't."

"Why not?"

"They don't teach foreign language at the alternative school."

Rose and Grandmother exchanged glances.

"Do you like that school?" Monica asked TJ.

"Yes," TJ said. "The students and staff respect each other."

This was true.

TJ looked at me. "You won't be able to stay in the Coop very long if you're going to be a linguist."

"If I ever get to be one."

Grandmother dipped a piece of turkey into her cranberry sauce. "Not *if*. *When*."

"Oh, yes. *When.* You have to understand Grandmother, TJ. She believes you make up your own life."

"She does that to you, too, Didi?" Rose asked. "I remember when I was ten I had to say, 'When I am a gymnast.' "

"*When* I am a fashion model," Cindy said loudly, through a mouthful of mashed potatoes.

"If that's what you're going to be, you'll have to grow ten inches and not gain a pound for the next eight years," I told her. "So you better push your plate away."

"Oh." She thought a minute. Then started scarfing her food down again. "I don't want to be a model *that* much."

Rose looked pensively at the yellow chrysanthemums in the center of the table. "This is the last time I'll be eating with you for another year."

"You're coming for Christmas," Dad asked.

Rose shook her head, waving her amber earrings. "Nope, this uses up my vacation time."

Cold fingers stroked my insides. "Grandmother! You're not leaving, too."

"I'll stay a couple more weeks if it'll help," she said to me.

I nodded. Anyway, I consoled myself, when Grandmother left, there'd be no reason to keep Monica.

TJ said his good-byes at six-thirty. I walked him out to the porch and slipped a picture into his hand. "Happy birthday, TJ."

He held it under the porch light. "I've never seen you in that outfit."

"Rose took it last week." I wrapped my arms around my shoulders. My silk dress wasn't much help in the freezing night air.

He kept studying the picture, and there was a tender, vulnerable look on his face I hadn't seen before. "You look like you belong on a stage." He carefully placed the picture in his jacket pocket. "You're shaking."

"You noticed."

"See you at the rehearsal tomorrow evening," he said, and tilted my chin and kissed me one stingingly sweet kiss good night.

Ten

The rehearsal was in Joe's basement. Stacy and I got there while TJ was singing, so we joined Larry, who was sitting on a tattered couch smoking weed. Singing got TJ high. He grabbed me when the music stopped and yelled, "Come on, let's rock and roll!"

"Hey, babe, show me how you do it." I swung around him, nipping at the back of his neck.

"I'll drink to that," TJ said, and steered me behind the drums where a case was stashed.

Joe raised up from fiddling with the foot pedal on his base drum. "That wasted thing is going to last about one more night." He looked at TJ. "I took a down payment to Kennelly Keys so they'd hold my new set. I should have the rest by next week. Did you call about the lessons?"

TJ took a swig from his bottle. "Not yet."

"When?" Joe asked.

"Real soon," TJ said. "I'm getting some extra bucks for overtime next payday."

"I know you've got more range. Let's get down to it." Joe searched around among the bottles in the case until he found a full one.

The lead guitar joined us and took the bottle from Joe's hand. Joe reached down for another one while the guitar player rocked his upper body as he drank his beer. I knew. He was hearing music in his head.

"Let's play 'Jump' next set," he said.

"Man, that song's so-o burned out." Joe was so-o crabby.

"You're so crabby, Joe," I told him.

"Damn right," Joe said. "I've put in enough time as a basement beater."

The guitar player was still jiggling. "Let's play 'Jump.' We played your tune last time, Joe."

Joe put his beer on the floor and picked up his sticks. "OK, but this is your last choice for tonight."

While the band played, two couples came down the steps into Joe's basement. I smiled a hello to Jamison's friend Craddoc. TJ called from the microphone to the redhead, "Hey, Jack!"

When the set was over, TJ introduced us around. Craddoc's girl was a blonde named Elsie Edwards. The girl with

Jack was Jenny Sawyer. Craddoc sat down on the edge of the couch and zeroed in on Stacy. "Seen Brian lately?"

Stacy shook her head. Larry eased over to the beer. He was wearing a black leather jacket I hadn't seen before. Craddoc glanced after him. "You into head-bangers now, Stacy?"

She shook her bowed head again, concentrating on peeling the label off the bottle she was holding. Elsie shot Craddoc an exasperated look and sat down on the other side of Stacy. Jack moved into the silence by asking TJ how he liked the Coop.

"Great," TJ said. "You get treated like a human being. How come you're still taking that shit Fircrest puts out?"

"Not for long," Jack said.

The two couples stuck around for another set. Jack waved to TJ when they left, and I heard Jenny say to Elsie, "Don't you think Stacy's changed?"

"Something's really wrong with her," Elsie answered.

After Joe's place folded, a bunch of us went over to TJ's. TJ had huge band posters on his walls. It was another basement room in an old house, but cheerful. *And* neat. Which surprised me. I thought he'd have dirty socks on the floor, empty beer cans, and dumped-over ashtrays.

I sat down with TJ on the long blue couch and looked around. "Where's your bed?"

"You're sitting on it." TJ reached between his feet and

pulled a lever. The couch began to slip under me. "More?"

"No! Not now."

"Later?"

Larry was on the floor, cleaning some more of his skunk weed.

Joe leaned down from his chair. "That better not be part of what you're supposed to be selling."

"No, no. Don't worry. I've got your take all put away."

"Where?" Joe asked him.

"At my house," Larry said. "Don't worry. You'll get yours."

"I better," Joe told him. "Monday."

I whispered to TJ, "Joe fronts Larry?"

TJ nodded.

Larry had been passing his bong around all evening. I was wondering where he got all the money for it. I was wondering where he got the money for what he and Stacy smoked up, too. That stuff's expensive and Larry doesn't work. The only other person I smelled it on was TJ.

"I bet Larry smoked up all Joe's front money," I whispered to TJ.

TJ shrugged.

After Joe and the band members left, Larry filled his bong again, and he and Stacy ended up crashed on the floor. TJ nudged them over by the chairs and pulled the couch out.

He turned the lamp off, reached out for me, and tumbled me into the bed beside him. It was so easy to wrap my arms around TJ's neck and to stretch my body against his as he kissed me. So easy to sink in the bed under him and let everything float away.

TJ's kisses traveled down my neck, and I felt my muscles loosen. . . . I slipped my fingers over his lips. He shook his head free.

"No, TJ, wait a minute. I should tell you something."

"What?" TJ's breath came in heaves.

"TJ, I should tell you I'm a virgin."

TJ hovered above me. "Are you saving it for something special?"

"Are you special?"

"Tonight I'll be special." He sank down beside me, and while he held me, he undid the top buttons of my blouse and pressed his mouth against me.

I pulled at his head. "TJ, wait a minute. Wait a minute."

"What?" TJ said.

"I'm not on the pill or anything."

TJ flopped over on his back and groaned loudly, "Didi!"

That roused Stacy. She sat up. "What time is it?"

Larry peered at his watch. "One-forty."

"Oh, God, I've got to go." I sat up and buttoned my blouse.

TJ rolled off the bed. "You going over to Stacy's?"

"No, Stacy's coming to my house, huh, Stacy?"

"OK," Stacy said, and looked happy for the first time that night.

Monday morning at the break, Larry was going on and on about how somebody snuck in his house and ripped off all the money he had stashed away for Joe. I wondered if Joe would buy that story.

He didn't. Joe told Larry he had a week to come up with the money or he'd beat the shit out of him. Larry kept explaining that it wasn't his fault, he got ripped off. Joe poked Larry in the chest, said, "You got a week," and walked away.

Larry turned back to us and started explaining all over how carefully he had saved Joe's money and hidden it in his room. If I were Larry, I'd have been worried. TJ said when Joe loses it, he busts everything in sight.

At the end of the break Rita came out from the back of the basketball court and swung by us. We followed her down to the home ec room. "That's one crispy chickie," TJ said.

Right.

The home ec class was taught by Ellen. Larry had made it out of orientation by then and was in there, too. Ellen put us in little cooking groups. Stacy, me, Larry, and a girl named Peggy were in one. We drew straws for who'd do the cooking and who'd do the cleaning up. I got stuck with the first cleaning. Larry got stuck with Tuesday's. The bad thing about it was being late for lunch. Stacy bought mine for me so I wouldn't risk being at the end of the line when the food ran out.

On Tuesday we were at a table together when Larry came in. He didn't seem to mind getting a half-frozen corn dog and warm chocolate milk. While he ate, he entertained us with tales of the training school. We were almost finished eating when Peggy rushed up to our table.

"Larry, did you lock the home ec room?" she asked.

"Sure," Larry said. "I gave the key to Ellen in the faculty room."

"I think that's where I left my purse. Did you see a purse in there?"

"I was at the sink doing dishes. I didn't see no purse. Where'd you leave it?"

"Hanging over my chair, I think. Oh, God, I cashed my paycheck last night and all my money's in it. Are you sure you didn't see it?"

"No. Ask the new orientation kids. Sometimes they come through the inside doors when they smell food."

"Oh, God!" Peggy turned and rushed back out.

While we were dumping our trays into the garbage can, Ellen came into the gym, tapped Larry on the shoulder, and told him Ruth, the principal, wanted to see him.

"What for?" Larry wanted to know.

"Peggy lost two weeks' pay out of her purse and you were the last one in the home ec room."

"I don't know nothin' about her purse. I was just doing the dishes."

"Maybe you can help us figure out if anybody else came in the room. Let's go talk to Ruth." Ellen kept right beside Larry as they walked out the door and toward the office.

After typing, I passed Larry on the walkway between the buildings. "Peggy find her money?"

"I don't know," Larry said. "Ruth accused me and made me take off my shoes and socks and turn my jacket inside out."

"Did Ruth find any money on you?"

"She didn't find nothin'. I didn't rip off that stupid chick."

Eleven

Larry's week was up on December 9. I went to school that Monday wondering if Joe would waste him, but they were playing Frisbee together at the morning break. "Looks like Joe got paid," I said to TJ. "Do you think Larry did take the money out of Peggy's purse?"

TJ just raised one eyebrow.

Still watching the game, Stacy asked me, "Can you stay at my house Friday night?"

It was the last thing I wanted to do. I looked for help from TJ, but he said, "I have to work this weekend."

"OK, I guess I can stay with you," I told Stacy. "Only I'll have to get home early in the morning because Grandmother is leaving."

I dawdled as long as I dared before showing up at Stacy's on Friday. Mr. Reynolds was in the living room sucking on a can of beer when I went through on the way to Stacy's bedroom. "Your dad gives me the creeps," I told Stacy.

"Gives *you* the creeps," she said.

He was at the breakfast table the next morning. It made me jumpy to sit down with him. He eyed Stacy and me sourly. "You girls got something going together?"

I stopped with my bite of French toast halfway to my mouth. "What?"

"Stacy has to run over to your house one week to sleep in your bed. You have to come over here the next week to get in her bed."

I put my fork down and stared at him, stunned. Then I stared at Stacy. Her skin had turned blotchy red. She wouldn't look at me, but kept her face hung down with her long hair shielding her eyes.

Mr. Reynolds leaned forward. "Well, what's going on with you two?"

Mrs. Reynolds fluttered around the table. "Ken, I don't think—"

He gave *her* a look.

"We're friends," I said.

He pushed his lips up under his mustache. "I had *friends* when I was your age. I don't remember hopping in their beds every night."

What could I say? I couldn't say I only came over so Stacy'd feel OK coming to my house. I couldn't say since the night I'd heard him beat on his wife I hated to come over. I sat there.

Mr. Reynolds kept eyeing me while he took a gulp of his coffee. "Well? Don't you think it looks funny?"

When I get a little mad, I say things. When I get medium mad, I kick things. But when I get real mad, my body goes on automatic and I talk slow and low and what comes out comes out of an icy heat.

I folded my napkin carefully and rose from the table. "I understand clearly that I am not welcome here."

I walked into Stacy's bedroom, gathered up my night things, walked back through the living room and out the door. There hadn't been a sound in the house.

I don't remember the walk home. It seemed as if I were propelled on legs that weren't mine. I went into Mother's old room and paced around. I sat on her bed and picked at the flowers on her quilt. I stayed there until I heard Grandmother's voice in the hall. "Has Didi come home yet?"

"I'm here," I called, and got up from my mother's bed.

Dad was carrying Grandmother's luggage out to her car. She put her arm around me as if to walk me out behind him. I slowed her pace. "Grandmother, maybe I should come with you."

"Oh, you'll be fine, honey. I'll miss you, but I'm too old for a teenager again." She kissed me on the forehead. "Come on. I want to get an early start."

After she hugged Dad at her car door, she turned with

her arms out to me. I went to her. "Grandmother, you're coming back for Christmas?"

"No, love, I'm worn to the bone. But I have a special present I'll mail you."

I felt my face crumple. "Grandmother, I don't think—"

She wiped my tears away with her gloved hand. "It just takes a while, dear. You and your dad are going to be fine." She kissed me good-bye then and climbed into her car.

I leaned against my dad, watching her drive away. Maybe I'll be all right with him, I thought as we walked together back to the house. Maybe I'll get to know him. It had always been Mother and me. Maybe if I gave him a chance. After all, Grandmother loves him.

Those nice thoughts melted away with the sound of the kitchen door opening. "Who's that?" I asked, and went to see.

Monica and her daughter Cindy were lugging two suitcases across the kitchen floor.

"What are you doing here?" I asked Monica. "I thought you'd be leaving."

"Whoever said that?" Monica wheezed, and put down the suitcase she was carrying.

"I'm moving in, too," Cindy crowed. "We saw your grandmother pull out. We get her room."

"What?!"

I found Dad in the living room figuring in his checkbook. "What's this about Cindy moving in here?"

He looked up. "Monica said she had to use most of her pay for baby-sitting, so it seemed like a sensible solution."

"To what?" I asked. "We don't need Monica now." And I didn't buy that baby-sitting story, either. I'd heard Monica tell Cindy to be nice to me or they'd be sleeping on her grandma's living-room couch forever.

Dad went on explaining. "Monica was worrying, so I reassured her she was welcome to stay until she finds another job. Somebody's got to cook."

"Cook! She can't cook!"

"I think she tries hard."

"Dad, I can cook as good as Monica."

"You have your schoolwork to do. Anyway, it's settled for now." He gave his attention back to his checkbook, and I knew I wasn't going to get any more out of him.

Monica and Cindy came into the living room after dinner to watch TV. A thing they'd never done before. Cindy chose an old movie with Shirley MacLaine. I had nothing else to do, so I watched it with them until the young mother in the movie got cancer. My impulse was to get up and go to my room, but I stayed. Lonely, I guess.

I was OK until the young mother's children were brought into her hospital room for a final good-bye. As the scene hit me, I opened my mouth for air, but my chest squeezed in, preventing me from taking a breath. "Maybe we'd better turn that off," I heard Dad say.

"No-o," Cindy objected. "I want to see how it ends."

Monica looked from Dad to me, concern spreading

across her face. "Turn it off," she told Cindy.

I got up and backed out of the room. Dad rose to follow. I put up both my hands. "No!" Upstairs I huddled on my bed with the knuckles of my fingers pressed into my mouth. I wasn't ever again going to have a mother. She was *dead*.

Later, when I heard Monica bring Cindy up to bed, the tears came, slid down my cheeks, and wet my pillow. I'd shut Dad out when he tried to come to me, and he must hurt, too. Maybe if we could sit together for a while it would feel better.

I slipped off the bed and, still clutching a wad of wet Kleenex, I padded downstairs. Outside the door of the living room, I stopped. Monica's voice drifted out. "I feel sorry for Didi, too, but I feel sorrier for you. She has her life in front of her. You've lost your mate."

"But maybe if I'd been a different man, Anne would have had a reason to live."

Monica's voice was vehement. "Oh, that's rubbish. You can't believe that mumbo jumbo."

"I don't know." Dad's voice was losing the dull, depressed tone. "I didn't consider her feelings very often."

"You gave her a beautiful house . . ."

I turned and trod slowly upstairs. Dad was talking more to Monica than he had talked to me in fifteen years. She would convince him he was a big man, cancer was a virus. Who wanted to believe in Grandmother's hard responsibility? And Monica was soft. Fat, squishy, baby-powdery soft.

When I was back under my covers, the picture of Mother's gray face against the white pillow floated in my head. The two spots of rouge on her cheeks reminded me of the only time I heard her and Dad quarrel.

The clerk in Dad's pharmacy was ill, and Mother offered to come in and run the cash register. Dad agreed, mostly because it was vacation time and there was no one else he could hire.

Mother bustled off to work each morning and bustled in each night, bringing frozen food for dinner. When Dad's clerk, Mrs. Botts, got well, Mother said why didn't she stay on running the cash register so Mrs. Botts could keep the stock on the shelves. Dad didn't like the idea at all, and when Mother kept on him, he told her, "No, I can't have you in there. You chat too much."

"How can you say I *chat*? I try to be pleasant to the customers so they'll come in again."

"Nobody wants to hear what a pretty color their blouse is when their hemorrhoids hurt. They want to get home and use the medicine."

My parents were standing in the middle of the living room while the argument went on. I was reading in the big chair and they didn't notice me, but I saw Mother's flaming cheeks and felt sorry for her, even though I knew she always fell all over herself about "such a pretty skirt" or "what a pretty scarf."

Poor lonely Mama. I lay there remembering how she liked pictures and flowers. Especially blue irises. I counted all the nice things she had done for me and all the things I wished I'd done for her.

It was after midnight. There was no chance for sleep. I pulled my body up on my hands and knees, my damp hair swinging over my wet pillow. TJ. If I could get to TJ, TJ would hold me, TJ would comfort me.

I got out of bed, put on my coat and moccasins, went downstairs and out the back door. I just kept going. Down the sidewalks, across the streets, the two miles to TJ's place.

His door wasn't locked. I crept through his dark room and stumbled on the edge of his bed. He awoke with a jerk.

"It's me," I said, and crawled in next to him.

He put his arms around me and held me close. "How'd you get here?"

"I walked here."

"Something happen?"

"Everything. Stacy's dad doesn't want me around her, my dad's getting consoled by the idiot housekeeper, my mother's dead, and Grandmother doesn't want me with her, either."

TJ burrowed his face into my neck. "I want you."

"I know, but . . . I still don't have anything and I just need you to hold me."

He raised up. "I've got something."

I pulled him back down. "No, TJ, just hug me. I hurt."

He hugged me for a while, but his body moved by itself and he drew away. "Maybe we should go for a walk."

"I don't want to walk. I've already walked. Can't you hold me?"

"Yes, but, Didi—"

"Oh, you don't have to." I got out of bed quickly and slipped into my coat and shoes.

"Wait a minute. I'll go with you."

"I'll go by myself." I flew out of there and started down the street, fast. I ran through alleyways I knew he wouldn't expect me to and across backyards and into my back door. I went up to my room and waited.

Stones trickled down my window. I listened to him try the door, circle around the house, and call out below my bedroom. I watched him a long time from behind my curtains, my body shaking and my mouth pulled into a bitter grin. I hoped it was good and cold out there.

Twelve

TJ *tried to call me twice on Sunday, but I hung up the* phone. When my bus pulled into the Coop the next morning, he was waiting. I walked on by. He caught up with me in the court and took me by the arm.

"Give me a chance to explain, Didi."

"You don't have to explain anything." I tried to wrench away from him.

He held on. "Just listen a minute."

"I don't want to hear all your excuses. I wanted you to comfort me awhile. That was too much to ask, right?"

"No, Didi, listen—"

"I don't wanna listen. I already know what you'll tell me. You'll say you got horny, right?"

"Well, that's part of it—"

"That's all of it. What about me? My mother's dead. What about me?" I knew I was screaming.

TJ looked around at all the kids staring at us. "Didi, cool it a little."

"You cool it. Cool it and get away from me."

He did.

Stacy tried to talk to me afterwards in David's class. She tried to tell me I shouldn't be so hard on TJ. She said I didn't understand about emotions.

"You do?" I asked her. "A male can't come within ten feet of you."

"I know about men," she said evenly. "And TJ's a nice one."

"Well, he wasn't nice to me." I walked over and watched the chess game until David came up behind me and put his arm around my shoulders. "Having a bad day today, Didi?"

I blinked fast to keep the tears from sliding down my cheeks. It was easier when no one felt sorry for me.

In the night, when I calmed down, the guilt seeped in, and I hated myself for taking my misery out on TJ. I tried to soothe myself by promising to see him as soon as I got to school. I imagined I would walk up casually and say, "I guess I've been pretty upset lately . . ." or "I guess I've been pretty hard to get along with lately . . ."

Only TJ wasn't at school the next day. Or the next day. I kept rehearsing my speech, but TJ didn't come. Stacy's

Aunt Katherine was having a Christmas sale at her florist shop and wanted Mrs. Reynolds to work Wednesday, Thursday, and Friday. It was OK with me for Stacy to stay over since I was lonesome, anyway. We played tunes most of the night.

The next Friday when I got home after school, Cindy was sitting at the kitchen table stuffing her face.

"Where'd you get that cake?" I asked her.

"It's ours. Mom bought it."

"With whose money?"

"Who cares?"

"When's your mother getting another job?"

"I don't know." Cindy picked up the cutting knife and licked the frosting off.

Monica came through the kitchen door and took the knife away. "You be careful or you'll get fat."

"Fat-ter," I corrected her, and went to answer the ringing phone.

It was Stacy. She wanted to know if it was OK to stay all night again. Monica was lurking around the phone, trying to act like she wasn't listening, so I just said sure.

When I hung up, Monica asked, "Who was that?"

"A friend."

That didn't satisfy her. She had to add, "I hope you're not having Stacy here again."

"What difference does it make to you? This isn't your house."

She complained to Dad at dinner. She said Stacy and I

played music all night and kept Cindy awake and Cindy was little and needed her sleep.

Cindy looked up from her plate. "I never hear anything."

"Well, I do," Monica said. "I don't know why that girl has to be here every week."

"She doesn't," Dad said. "Cut out the all-night visits, Didi."

"She hasn't been here since last Friday," I said. "And I already promised—"

"No more nights."

"But her dad—"

"*No* more nights."

That was it. I called Stacy after dinner and told her she couldn't come.

The next morning, Dad gave Monica a bunch of money for Christmas buying, and she must have bought out the town. The house was decorated up like a store window by Saturday night.

"Look at the presents already, Didi." Cindy pointed to the packages under Monica's plastic tree. "You know, a funny thing happened when we got in Mom's car to go shopping. The car smelled like perfume."

"It smelled like your friend," Monica said, sorting through the new boxes of baubles. "I hope she isn't using my car for her bed."

I waited until Monica went to the kitchen to warm up the Kentucky Fried Chicken for dinner before I phoned Stacy. "Are you all right?" I asked her.

"Why?" she said.

"Somebody was in Monica's car last night."

"Was anything taken?" she asked after a minute.

"No."

"That's good. I'll catch ya later."

Monica locked her car up tight before she went to bed. I hoped it wasn't Stacy who'd been in there. She didn't talk to me much at school Monday. Mostly because she was fried. TJ didn't come to school.

When Stacy got off the bus Tuesday morning, she headed right for the back of the basketball court. I tagged after her. Larry was sharing again. As he passed the bong around, he kept alert for the approach of any faculty member by swiveling his eyes back and forth.

"Larry," I asked, hesitating only a moment before I took a hit, "how come you never turn your head when you're watching for someone?"

"You'd know if you'd ever been in lockup," he said. "You don't go craning your head around there. They slapped one of the guys in solitary for staring at a Christmas tree. They figured he was planning on busting the glass ornaments."

"That's barbaric!"

Larry gave a bitter laugh.

"What's solitary like?" I wondered.

"Like a meat locker. The can's bolted to the floor and so is the bed. There's an intercom on all the time. In the night you don't want to open your eyes because it's so dark in there you can't make out your hand in front of your face." Larry reached over and took the bong away from Stacy and stashed it under his jacket just before David called across the court, "Come on, you guys. Let's go to class."

Two students just out of orientation were standing in the middle of David's room. When they sat down, they sat next to Peggy and one of her straight friends. I felt David watching us. Sort of the same as I'd seen him watching Rita. I ducked my head down when he headed for our table. Larry moved over to give David room to pull out a chair.

"We ain't botherin' nobody," Larry told him.

"Just kickin' back listening to the lights hum?" David said. "You can do that at home. What's the point of coming to school?"

"I have to," Larry said. "My PO makes me."

David thoughtfully traced his finger over the cover of the book he'd brought with him. "I don't know, Larry. I think maybe you'll have to do more than just show up at school to make it on the outside." He pushed the book along the table toward me. "This is by Oliver LaFarge, Didi. He understood the Indian culture. I thought you might enjoy reading it after *Black Elk*."

"Thanks," I told him. I flipped through the pages of the book and stopped at the picture of Indians working their own plantations. Indians owned plantations? When we picked up our things to go to home ec, I forgot the book and left it on the table.

Halfway through lunch I got so sleepy I wondered to Stacy how I was going to make it through the typing class.

Rita was sitting across from us. "I can fix you up if you've got a dollar."

"I've got a dollar," Stacy said.

She pulled the dollar out. Rita took it and passed me the tab. I swallowed it down with my milk.

By fifth period I was flying. The typing teacher never noticed. She belonged in a regular school. If any students bothered her by asking for help, she told them to read their manual. I whizzed through three keyboard exercises and turned them in. Leaving the teacher puzzling over my typing, I went to find Stacy in art.

Simon was at his desk arguing with Dianna, who had come for his monthly attendance record. "It has to be turned in today," Dianna was insisting.

"If Ruth wants it today, tell her to come over and take my class for an hour. I can't be with kids every minute and do paperwork, too." There was irritation in Simon's voice I hadn't heard before.

My attention shifted to a new boy in a navy blue ski sweater who was sitting at the table beside Stacy. He was carefully coiling strips of clay around the top of a large pot. I leaned on the table. "Where is the cobra and where is the flute? Here, I'll help you."

I smashed the heel of my hand on a rope of clay he had prepared and formed a wedge-shaped head, forked tongue, and two eyes out of the smashed end. Dangling the snake above the pot, I hesitated. "No, it would look better peeking out of the side." With my index finger I poked a hole in the side of the pot.

The boy pulled back in his chair, wrinkling his nose as if I smelled bad. "Simon," he called, "get this druggie away from me."

Simon turned from his argument with Dianna. Before he could move toward us, I waved. "Just leaving."

Outside the art room, I swung around the posts at the edge of the covered walk, trying to shake the boy's disgust from my head. Around and around, Grandmother's voice followed me. "And are you going to like what you are making and are you going to like what you are making and are you going to like what you are making . . ." Peggy came along the walk, gave me a small, secret smile, and asked how I was doin'. OK, I guessed, and swung the other way.

She was the one who'd convinced Stacy that completing David's forty questions was a faster way to make a credit than reading another book. They were values questions about what you thought of your family and your neighborhood and drugs and the schools and the government.

When Stacy handed in her stack of papers, David called her up to his desk to complain. "Stacy, I'm not satisfied with these answers."

"What's wrong with my answers?"

"I don't know any more about you than before I read them."

Stacy pointed her finger at her papers on David's desk. "Your directions say to answer each question in one hundred words or more. I did that."

"I know, but . . ." David picked up a paper. "Here. I asked you to describe your family and how you see your place in it, and you wrote about your family tree."

"So-o?" Stacy said. "What did you want me to say?"

"For example, how do you relate to your other family members?"

Stacy's eyes narrowed. That's the one question she hates.

David put the paper down. "Stacy, I don't understand you any better than before I read this."

"Is prying part of your job description?"

Chills went up my arms. The dream. Rita was sleeping. Joe and Larry were playing chess. Stacy was arguing with David.

"Stacy!" I said after class. "That fight you had was the same as in my dream!"

But Stacy was on her own track. "I never asked David to understand me."

I heard her say that again at a party the Saturday night before Christmas. Rita's mother was on the town again, and half of Cooperation was at her house. Stacy and I were sitting at our old place under the fern by the wall, watching the crowd mill. We were both blitzed, and it kept passing through my mind that TJ might come in. TJ didn't come in. But Brian did.

I was wondering who that big dude with the shoulders was, when he turned around. "Brian," I whispered.

Stacy already knew. I could tell by the way she was concentrating on her fingernail polish.

Brian walked right up. "Hello, Stacy."

Stacy looked up slowly. Pink ran down her cheeks onto her throat. "Hello, Brian."

"Can I sit with you?" he asked, and before Stacy could answer he sat on the floor beside her. "Is this where you hang out now?"

"One of the places," Stacy said.

He watched her closely. "You come with someone?"

"No."

I leaned my head back against the windowsill. The room looked like a scene through a kaleidoscope. "Cartoon land," I mumbled to Stacy. She nodded.

"What was that?" Brian asked.

Neither of us answered.

He put his hand on Stacy's arm. "How about going for a ride with me?"

She shook her head.

"Do you have somebody new, Stacy?"

"No."

"Did I do something to you I don't know about?"

She shook her head again.

"You know, Stacy, you're not helping me to understand you."

"I don't remember asking you to understand me." She rose to her feet. "We have to go. Come on, Didi."

I followed her through the crowd, out the door, and into the rainy night. We walked block after block in the rain. When we crossed the streets, the distant sound of cars ballooned in my ears and sent me skittering to the curb.

"It would have been a lot easier to have gone with Brian," I complained to Stacy. "What happened between you and him? I remember when I walked in on you at a party you were sure getting off on each other."

"That must have been before my dad got back."

"The next time I saw you, Brian was having a fit. What did you do to him out in the garden?"

"I just didn't want to be pawed, that's all."

"You mean Brian never 'pawed' you before?"

She hurried ahead of me. I caught her arm, slowing her down. "Stacy, sometimes do you miss Brian? I miss TJ."

"You were mean to TJ," Stacy said.

"I know. I was passing my misery around. Do you wish you were back with Brian?"

"I can't be with anyone."

"Why not?"

She didn't answer.

I pulled on her arm. "Stacy, why not?"

She plowed on ahead.

I yanked her to a stop. "Stacy! Why not?"

"Because of my father. Because who would want me?"

"I don't get it."

"Because my father's had me."

"He what?"

"My father gets in my bed."

"What?"

"You heard me."

I dropped her arm. "You *did* sleep in my garage, didn't you? Oh, no . . ." It hit me and I backed away, holding my stomach.

"That's exactly why I never told you." She didn't sound like a friend.

"Oh, no. No. I feel terrible because I left you out there. Because I didn't help you more."

"Who would want to?"

"I would want to. And David would. And probably Madge. And even Brian."

"Forget it, Didi."

I took Stacy's hand. "Why don't you tell Madge? She'll know what to do."

"I said forget it." She yanked her hand away. "Do you know what he'd do if he found out I told?"

"Oh, Stacy. Anyway, remember we're friends." I reached for her hand again and felt it gradually relax in mine as we walked along. When we got in front of her house, I couldn't help asking, "What was it like?"

"Pukey."

110:

"Well, what *are* you going to do?"

"I'm taking off after Christmas."

"Where will you go?"

"I don't know, but I'm going."

"Maybe if you told your mother . . ."

"No, I've gone through every 'maybe' a million times, and he's told me a million times that he'll let her starve if I tell her. I just have to get out of here."

"If only . . ."

" 'If only's don't do me any good," Stacy said. "I'll catch ya later."

I watched her go over the grass and up to her door. I wanted to run after her and say, "Come with me," but I couldn't. Or say, "We'll run away together," but I didn't know where.

Thirteen

Rose always sends me money for Christmas, and I use that for my shopping. By Christmas Eve I had wrapped my presents and put them under the tree. A plastic tree doesn't seem right to me. Mother always had a live tree that Dad planted in our yard after New Year's. But I was trying hard not to let little things bother me. I wanted Christmas, anyway.

Monica said we should dress for Christmas Eve dinner. I wore my ecru wool dress. Monica wore a long red dress of some sleazy material. It was cut low in front and she modestly held her hand over the neckline as she bent forward to sit in her chair. There was a bottle of wine in front of Dad's plate.

"I thought I'd let you do the wine honors," Monica said to him when we were all seated.

"Oh, yes, of course," he said as if he were used to assuming that responsibility. He rose from the table and opened the bottle with the fancy corkscrew that Monica had put beside it. First he filled Monica's glass, and then he turned to me. There was no wineglass at my plate. "Aren't you joining us tonight, Didi?" he asked.

I got up to get myself a glass, but Monica held out a hand. "Oh, I don't think the girls should be drinking." She patted Cindy's arm.

Dad looked uncertain for a minute and then sat down and filled his own wineglass.

I felt my face flame. Don't lose it, I told myself. Don't lose it. Tomorrow's Christmas.

I woke up early in the morning, like I always do on Christmas. I knew it wasn't going to be the same, but I was excited, anyway.

Cindy squealed when she saw the ten-speed bike under the tree. That must have cost a bit, I thought to myself. I glanced over the packages to see if I could figure out what my big present would be.

Monica said Dad should be Santa Claus.

"Me first! Me first!" Cindy begged, bouncing around on the floor.

I sat in a chair, waiting.

Dad read the tag on the bike. "I guess Santa brought you this, Cindy."

Cindy wheeled the bike out from under the tree and stroked the shiny handlebars. I remembered how excited I was with my first bike. I smiled up at Dad.

"Let's see." He examined the names on the packages in front of the tree. "What's Santa got here for Didi? Well, Monica, I guess you can be next." He handed Monica a large envelope.

Monica tore it open and pulled out the pharmacy Christmas card. A check fluttered to the floor. She stooped to pick it up.

"How much is it?" Cindy stared over Monica's shoulder at the amount on the check. "Wow! That's neat. What are we gonna buy?"

Monica looked at Dad with widened eyes.

He waved his hands disparagingly. "Everybody at the pharmacy got a turkey bonus, but I thought you could use a little extra cash."

"Oh, yes," Monica said breathlessly. "Oh, thank you, Raymond." She got up from her chair with her arms outstretched, but catching Dad's startled look, she sat down again quickly.

"Now give him yours," Cindy directed her mother.

Keeping her reddened face lowered, Monica went to the tree, lifted up a square package, and handed it to Dad. He undid the bow and took a man's travel case from the box. "Thank you, Monica. I can certainly use this." He carefully loosened the stopper of the after-shave lotion to smell the fragrance.

"Come on, you guys. Pass out some more presents," Cindy said. "Give Didi one."

Dad looked over the present tags again. He discovered one with my name on it under a pile to the side of the tree.

I unwrapped the Woolworth Christmas tree paper and found a cardboard checker-game.

"Do you like it? Do you like it?" Cindy hovered over me. "I thought we could play it together."

"It's great," I told her. "I'll play you a game after breakfast."

The next three presents were games for Cindy. Then Monica got a purse from her mother with a ten-dollar bill in it. Cindy gave Monica a pink bracelet and Dad opened the present from me. He said he could certainly use the leather key case I'd gotten him. I smiled and nodded, although my face was getting a bit stiff.

Finally I got another package. It was from Grandmother. A blue leather shoulder bag large enough for overnight trips. There was a light blue nightie tucked in it and a journal with blank pages for dreams.

The next two presents were clothes for Cindy. Dad got a set of books from Grandmother. There was nothing from the other grandparents. Maybe they weren't up to Christmas. Monica said she liked the silver earrings I bought her. I told her I liked the green frog pin with the yellow glass eyes she gave me. I pinned it on my nightgown and hoped I wouldn't have to wear it again.

Cindy put one of the tapes I gave her on the stereo, and

I sat in the middle of the blast of music looking at the rumpled wrappings. Christmas was over. I picked up the shoulder bag and the checkerboard and said, "Well, thanks, everybody. I better go over to Stacy's and give her my present."

Dad gave a quick glance at the empty floor around the Christmas tree. "Uh . . . I guess . . ." He pulled out his wallet and took out two twenties. "How about a little bonus for you? I guess I was pretty rushed this week."

I accepted the money, although I didn't really want to.

"And how would you like to go to the Space Needle with me for Christmas dinner?"

"That would be nice," I said.

"The Space Needle!" Cindy yelped. "Are we all going?"

"I've never been to the Space Needle," Monica put in. "I could use my Christmas money for Cindy's and my dinner."

"No," Dad said. "I'll treat everyone. How about it, Didi?"

"You all go," I told him. "I have to get over to Stacy's to give her my present."

"Aren't you going to help me ride my bike?" Cindy asked me.

"Dad'll help you," I said, and got out of there.

Stacy was gathering up her pile of presents when I arrived at her house, and after we exchanged ours, I helped her carry them to her bedroom. She asked me how Christmas was at my place, and I told her, "It wasn't. Let's go see what's going on at Rita's."

Rita welcomed us at the door with a big "Merry Christmas!" Larry was there and TJ and Peggy and a couple of kids I didn't know. Rita introduced us to her mother, who was friendly—and drunk. TJ was keeping her company.

"Merry Christmas," I said to him. I wanted so bad to reach out and touch him, but after he gave me a wan smile, he turned back to Rita's mother.

Peggy greeted me, and I told her I hadn't expected to see her there.

"Have you ever been in a foster home for Christmas?" A mean glint came into Peggy's eyes. "Larry got busted for Christmas."

Stacy and I settled on the floor next to him. "You got busted?"

"Those stinkin' cops. They accused me of trying to pawn a hot tape deck. How'd I know it was hot? I ain't going to show up in court. You got any money?" he asked me.

"What for?"

Larry pulled out an eighth and laid it in my lap. "You can have it for twenty bucks. I need gas money."

"Gas for what?" Peggy said. "A hot car?"

"My uncle's car. I can borrow it while he's in Hawaii. I got more brains than to take off in a hot car."

Peggy put on her coat. "If you had any brains, you'd take them out and play with them."

She left and I gave Larry a twenty and he lit up his bong. We passed it around, except TJ and Rita's mother didn't take any. They were sticking to booze.

Joe came in about a half hour later. He bumped into Stacy, who was heading for the john. "Well, spacy Stacy, all fried out."

"How's the new band?" TJ asked him.

"Tight. We're playing Saturday night, and an agent from Far West is coming to hear us."

"Excellent," TJ said. Rita's mother filled his glass.

Joe's starting a new band was sad for TJ, and I hurt for him. I knew TJ would never save his money for singing lessons, but it was still sad to be left behind. I turned my head toward Larry. "Where're you heading?"

"Nevada," Larry said. "My brother's down there. I'll stay with him until I get a job."

"Nevada?" I looked up at Stacy, who was back from the john. "Nevada? You want to go to Nevada?"

"Sure." Stacy settled on the floor.

"Where in Nevada?" I asked Larry.

"Reno," Larry said.

"Shall we go with him, Stacy?"

"Sure," Stacy said.

"When are you leaving?"

"Tonight," Larry said. "Have you got any more money?"

"Twenty dollars."

"You got any money, Stacy?" Larry asked her.

Stacy thought a minute. "About seventeen dollars, counting my Christmas money."

"That ain't enough. Listen." He lowered his voice. "I'll meet you at one o'clock in the parking lot at Haggen's. Only get at least a hundred."

"I don't think I can," I said.

"Your folks'll be asleep. Easy."

I got up unsteadily to go to the bathroom. On the way back I saw TJ had Stacy cornered by the front door. "He can't get his head out of his butt," TJ was saying. "All he thinks about is ripping off." When TJ saw me, he nodded at Stacy and went out the door.

"TJ doesn't think we should take off with Larry," Stacy told me.

"OK, then," I said, "what do you want to do?"

Stacy bit her fingernail. "I'm leaving, anyway. I'd just as soon go with Larry."

"Me, too."

Fourteen

Dad, Monica, and Cindy didn't get home until ten o'clock. I was getting a little jumpy by then. Cindy came into my bedroom to tell me about the movie they'd seen after their dinner. She started in on the whole plot until I told her I wanted to go to bed.

She hesitated at the door. "You know, Mom thought your dad was going to get your present and your dad thought my mom was going to get it. Pretty funny, huh?"

"Ya, pretty funny," I agreed.

Her face fell. "I didn't mean it was really funny. . . ."

"Good night," I told her.

I tried to read a book and listen to the sounds in the

120:

house at the same time. The bathroom was finally empty and the bedroom doors all closed at eleven o'clock. I let Stacy in the back door at eleven-thirty.

"Be real quiet," I said. "They've only been down a half hour."

We crept through the hall, and Stacy gave me her penlight out of her purse. I crept up to Dad's room. Larry's idea of easy isn't my idea of easy. I knew where Dad kept his wallet on top of the dresser, but getting money out of it in the dark while he was sleeping was scary. I fumbled around and dropped all his credit cards on the floor before I had my hands on the bills.

After closing his door softly, I turned and the tiny beam of the flashlight ran across the opposite wall and over the painting of the blue iris. I could hear Mother's voice: "Hold it up a little higher, Didi. No, down a little. Perfect. Let me mark the place. Isn't it beautiful, Didi?"

Sadness washed over me, coaxing me to sink onto the steps and cry. She'd had so many dreams for me, and if she could see me now . . . Clutching the banister to steady myself, I picked my way down the stairs to the living room and turned on the lamp on the telephone table.

"Only a minute," I told Stacy, who had followed me in, looking nervous, "I'm trying one last time."

I put the money and penlight on the table and dialed Grandmother's number. I swallowed before I answered her sleepy hello. "Grandmother? This is Didi."

"What time is it?"

"It's a little late." I swallowed again and then rushed on. "But guess what? That precognitive dream came true. About the ratty classroom. And it was Stacy who was having a fight with the teacher. And I know why she has a gray aura now. It's because her dad gets her in bed."

"That's sad to hear," Grandmother said.

"I got your present. The bag is neat. It's lucky you sent me something because that's all I got. Except he handed me some money afterwards." I had to stop a minute to wipe my eyes.

"Didi—" Grandmother's voice came over the receiver. "Didi, are you still there?"

"I'm still here. Grandmother, things . . . things aren't working out." I took a deep breath and held my hand over my face until I could force myself together. Stacy was sitting on the floor staring up at me. "Grandmother, could I please come live with you? I can't stay here."

"I love you very much, dear, but I'm not up to a teenager. I still haven't got my energy back from my visit up there."

"It seems like if you loved me, you'd want to help me. You took Dad when he was fourteen just because he wanted to go to a regular school."

"That was twenty-some years ago. I'm seventy-six years old now."

"Eighty-six is old. Seventy-six is *not* old. The way you get feeble is staying in your little house alone concentrating on being old. Isn't that the way your philosophy goes?" I stopped myself, dreading the silence on the other end. "I'm sorry, Grandmother. I don't mean to be rude. I'm really getting to know about what you mean about making your own reality. There's a boy here named Larry who's going to get himself sent back to reform school. But, Grandmother, we need someone to help us a little bit until we get older."

I waited through this silence with my hand back over my eyes. "I suppose," she said at last, "I could get a tutor so you could catch up on your languages."

My hand dropped to my side in relief. "I suppose you could call around tomorrow to find one."

"Well, give me a little time to get organized."

"You'll let me know as soon as you're ready? How long do you figure that will be?"

"I'll need to clean out the spare room and have it re-papered and put in a new bed. I should be ready in three or four weeks."

"Great. I'll tell Dad I'm moving in with you."

"No, you leave that up to me. I want to give him a call."

I loved the way she said that. He was going to get it.

I hung up the phone and squatted next to Stacy. "I did it! I did it! Stacy, she'll take me. I did it!"

"That's great," Stacy said quietly.

My bottom hit the floor with a thump. "Ohh, Stacy. What a pig I am. Your mess is worse than mine ever was."

Stacy's face crumpled as I reached out to hug her.

"Stacy, listen. We'll fix you up, too. When your mom works next week, I'll come stay with *you*. Then your dad can't get you. And the vacation will be over, and we'll talk to Madge before your mom works the next week."

Stacy pulled back.

"No, no. Listen, your dad will never find out we told until it's too late. Madge got Peggy a foster home."

"Don't be dumb, Didi. My dad isn't going to pay for me in a foster home."

"We'll think of something. I promise you. Just don't go with Larry, OK?"

Stacy sat there trying to blink her tears away.

"OK, Stacy?"

"OK," she said finally. "But what about the rest of tonight?"

"Let's go to bed. Monica can't do nothin' now."

I was almost asleep before the picture of the money sitting on the phone table floated through my mind. I ripped the covers off and made for the stairs. It was almost as hard getting the money back in as it was taking it out.

My hand knocked against Dad's keys when I reached for his wallet in the dark. As the keys scraped across the dresser, he turned over in bed with an "Unh, unh." I froze. When at last I heard a gurgling snore, I grasped the wallet, stuffed in the money, and got out of there.

Slipping past Stacy's dad on Friday night wasn't easy, either. I felt him following my steps across the living room with his mean little eyes. But the toughest thing of all was getting Stacy to help herself.

I had to push her to the door of Madge's office. And

after I got her there, she hesitated and then started down the hall. I grabbed her and pulled her back. Madge looked up from the tests she was scoring.

"Are you busy?" I asked.

"No, come on in."

I nudged Stacy forward.

Madge sat back in her chair. "What can I do for you two little devils?"

"I was wondering how many credits I have toward graduation," Stacy said.

I gave her a look, but she ignored me.

"Umm, I forgot your last name," Madge said.

"Stacia Reynolds."

Madge got up. "Just a minute. I'll get your folder."

So we had a conference on Stacy's credits. It was stupid.

"God, that was stupid," I told Stacy after we got out of there. I didn't think Madge was too bright, either. Did she really believe one girl would push another girl into her office to talk about credits?

When we passed through the main office, Dianna asked us how come we weren't in class.

"We were talking to Madge." I helped myself to the Reese's Pieces in the jar on Dianna's desk, and shared with Stacy.

"How are things going?" Dianna asked.

"OK." I opened the jar for more Reese's Pieces. "We got a friend who's having trouble, though."

"What's the matter with your friend?"

"Well . . . uh . . ." I looked at Stacy. Stacy was looking at the floor. "Well, her dad bothers her."

"How does her dad bother her?"

"He comes in her bedroom at night," I said.

"He only bothers her in her bedroom at night?"

"Yes."

"You're talking about incest," Dianna said.

"Yes," I said.

"How long has this been going on?"

"Well . . . uh . . ." I looked at Stacy. Stacy looked out the window. "About four months."

"Have you reported this to Child Protective or the police or told her mother?" Dianna asked.

Stacy started for the outside door.

"Hey, come back here," Dianna ordered.

Stacy came back.

"Now just a darn minute. This is serious. What are you girls going to do about this?"

"We don't know what to do," I told her. "If her dad gets mad at her mother, he'll beat her up. If the police make him leave, there won't be enough money."

"Go to DSHS," Dianna said.

"What's that?" I asked.

"The Department of Social and Health Services. Madge can explain it to you."

"Thanks. We'll tell our friend," Stacy said. "We'd better get back to class, Didi."

"Hold it, Stacy," Dianna said. "Have you got a lock on your bedroom door?"

"No," Stacy said.

"Is your bedroom on the first floor?"

"Yes," Stacy said.

"You get a lock on that door, and the first time your dad rattles that lock, you go out your window and call the police. You'll ruin your whole life if this goes on. What if you get pregnant? There's worse things than welfare, you know."

Stacy knew.

"You put a lock on your door, and if he touches it, you call the police."

"OK," Stacy said.

"You promise me?"

"Yes," Stacy said.

"Have you got money for a lock?"

"We can get it," I said.

"Today?" Dianna insisted.

"We'll get it today," I agreed.

"Stacy?"

"I promise," Stacy said.

As soon as we got out of the office, I asked Stacy, "Where are we going to get the money?"

Stacy put her books on the ground, took her wallet out of her purse, and counted her money. "I've got two dollars and twenty-three cents."

"I've got a dollar for lunch. That's over three dollars.

We should be able to buy a bolt for that."

Larry came swingin' by and tried to peer in our wallets. "I can get you some good coke."

"Get lost," I told him.

"Where were you guys? I waited two hours."

"We made other plans."

"Real nice of you to tell me."

It *was* kind of shitty. "Why didn't *you* go?" I asked him.

"Ran outta gas."

Fifteen

The bolt cost two dollars and ninety-seven cents. We stopped at the 7-Eleven on the way home from school and found it in a rack of kitchen utensils. Stacy soaped the screws like the clerk at the 7-Eleven told us to do. They went in pretty easy, considering that we were turning them with a kitchen knife. Stacy's dad was in the living room swilling beer, and we didn't want to get him suspicious by looking for his screwdriver.

When we finished screwing the lock to the door, we shoved the bolt in place and sat on Stacy's bed looking at it. I jumped when I remembered the phone call. "Stacy," I said, "the pay phone costs a quarter. Have you got a quarter left?"

She pulled the change out of her jacket pocket. She had two dimes and six pennies.

"Pennies won't do," I said. "Let's go back and change them for a nickel."

She thought a minute. "I think I have a buffalo nickel in my jewelry box."

She did. It was a shame to spend it, but I didn't say so. Instead I said, "Listen, when you go to call the police, call me first. Just let it ring once and hang up so you'll get your money back. I'll know it's you and come to the Seven-Eleven to meet you."

I expected the call on Friday, and it came about a quarter after eleven. I was half waiting and half dozing, and the sound startled me. I listened for a second ring. There was none.

When I got to the 7-Eleven, Stacy was leaning against the telephone booth, trying to shield herself from the winter sleet. We put our heads down and plowed against the wind to her house. A police car was parked out front.

"What are you going to tell them?" I asked.

"Nothing," she said. "My mom's in there. Let's get behind the bushes." We got behind the bushes and crouched there, shivering, peering between the leafless branches at Stacy's front door.

"When did your mom get home?"

"She got home early, about half-past ten. He was banging on my door and yelling at me to open it up."

"Well, what happened?" Stacy doesn't talk much, and when she does tell you something, she does it so darned slow.

"I heard her car drive up, and I thought maybe I wouldn't have to call the police. He kept yelling at me, and I heard her ask him what was going on. He told her to shut up. She asked him again why he was trying to get in my room, and he said, 'I told you to shut up,' and then she screamed, so I got out of there."

The front door to Stacy's house opened. I put my fingers in my mouth and bit on them.

A policeman stood in the lighted doorway. He seemed to be talking to someone inside the room. Another policeman came out on the porch with Mr. Reynolds. The two policemen steered Mr. Reynolds down the steps, each of them holding him up by an arm. He looked small and wimpy, sort of like a skinny doll between them. The policemen put him in the back of the patrol car and drove away.

"Let's go in," Stacy said.

I followed her slowly. This was a little much for me. We found Mrs. Reynolds huddled on the davenport, holding a towel over her bleeding mouth. Stacy took one look at her and went to the phone to call her aunt Katherine.

Katherine got Mrs. Reynolds cleaned up and all of us in the kitchen drinking coffee. "*This* time," she told Stacy's mom, "you file charges against him and get rid of him."

"He isn't all bad," Stacy's mother said.

"He's a vicious little pipsqueak," Katherine said.

Mrs. Reynolds stirred her coffee. I think it hurt her to drink it. "He's told me some sad stories about his father beating him."

"That's no excuse." Katherine turned to Stacy. "Why did you put a lock on your door?"

I could see Stacy was fumbling around in her mind for an answer, so I said, "For privacy."

"Oh, come on! He was after you, wasn't he, Stacy?"

She nodded. I was surprised she would.

"Why was he after you?" Katherine asked.

"Why do you think?" Stacy said.

Katherine blinked. I think she and Mrs. Reynolds figured, until that moment, that Mr. Reynolds was just going to hit Stacy, too.

"Dear God!" Mrs. Reynolds shuddered. She was a pretty sad-looking thing, sitting there with tears rolling down her battered face.

"Why didn't you tell us?" Katherine wanted to know.

"Because Dad said if I loved Mother I wouldn't tell her. And he said he'd let her starve if I did."

"Let's get straightened out here." Katherine's voice was loud. "Your mother has half of everything coming to her. This is a community-property state. Half of the house is hers, half of the bank account is hers, half of the furniture is hers. Half of everything. She is *not* going to starve. I wouldn't let her even if she didn't have any money. You, either. How could you be so dumb as to believe that?"

Easy, I thought.

Katherine's jaw jutted forward as she stared into Mrs. Reynolds's eyes. "Tomorrow you file charges against him. And you take Stacy."

Mrs. Reynolds nodded in agreement.

Stacy didn't come to school on Monday. I talked to her on the phone, and she said she and her mom spent half the morning being interviewed by a policewoman at the station. Stacy was in class Tuesday. As soon as we got together in the social studies room, David came up to us.

"You're looking a little better this week, Didi." He put his arm around me. He knew better than to put an arm around Stacy. "Why don't you two go down and talk to Madge a little while this morning?"

"What for?" I asked him.

"She'll tell you." He steered us back toward the door, past the chess game.

"Madge's probably been hearing things," Joe said, moving his bishop across the chessboard.

"What things?" I put my hands on my hips, then took them off quickly. I didn't want to look like Monica.

"Any *thing*." Joe lifted his finger off the chess piece. "That's mate."

"Wha-at?" Larry said.

When we poked our heads in her office door, Madge got up from her desk. "Come on in and sit down." She closed the door behind us. "Rumor has it that you two were thinking of running away. Bad things coming down on you, eh?"

"Not so bad now," I said.

"How about you, Stacy?"

"I think I'll be OK, too."

"What about your father?"

"I think he's in jail. Or was."

"Good," Madge said. "I received a call from a social worker at Child Protective yesterday. Are you going to get some counseling?"

"The policewoman said something about Harborview Medical Center having a group for kids who have been sex . . ." Stacy's voice dribbled off.

"They do have group therapy for victims of sexual abuse," Madge said. "It's a good idea. Sometimes girls think it only happens in their family or their family's weird or they're to blame."

Stacy's eyes were filling with tears.

"Do you think you were to blame?" Madge pulled a tissue out of a box on her desk and handed it to Stacy.

"This body doesn't help," Stacy said.

"Do you mean your body doesn't help because it was what tantalized your father?"

"That's mean," I objected.

Madge ignored me and kept her eyes on Stacy.

"Yes," Stacy said.

"Do you know girls three years old get abused, and the

average age is eleven years old? I doubt that your body had anything to do with your father's problem."

"Maybe not," Stacy said.

"It's really important for you to talk about your feelings with somebody. Would you let me call and get you an appointment?"

"The policewoman already did. I'm supposed to go today."

"Good. What time are you going?"

"At three. If I can get there."

"I'll take you, Stacy," I offered. "I'll show you how to go on the Metro. I'll go with you."

Madge smiled. There were tears in her eyes, too. I couldn't believe it.

Afterwards in the girls' john, while Stacy was splashing her face with water, I was still mumbling, "She had tears in her eyes. I can't believe it. This place is too much."

Stacy wiped the back of her hand across her wet face. "It's all right."

I cranked out the paper towels. "I guess."

Sixteen

In my last month at Cooperation High, I hardly saw TJ at school. Larry said TJ said chickies messed up his head. Larry disappeared permanently about two weeks before I left. Stacy told me Dianna said Larry got sent back up.

Stacy spent a lot of time sitting on the counter opposite Dianna's desk talking to her. Dianna and the group therapy started working on Stacy's head, and she got over the idea that what happened was her fault and no one would want her. I asked her if she thought she would get back with Brian.

"No," she said. "Brian would never understand."

"TJ would," I said.

"Yes, TJ would," she agreed. "Are you going to try to get back with him?"

"No use for a few weeks," I said, "but it's a temptation." I didn't add that it was a temptation every hour of the day.

Stacy didn't go behind the basketball court anymore. When she wasn't talking to Dianna, she was in David's room piling up the credits as fast as Peggy. She didn't know if her mother would take her dad back after he was "rehabilitated," or sell the house and put her half of the money into expanding the florist shop like Katherine wanted her to. Anyway, Stacy was getting out of high school and getting a job as quickly as she could.

At my house, Dad tried to smooth things over between us after he got Grandmother's call. He said he hoped I wasn't leaving because he goofed up Christmas. I said no, of course not. I was going to shorten up our little talk, but his face drooped with tired lines, so instead I told him I wanted to go to San Francisco to be with Grandmother and I would miss him when I was gone. I didn't know if the last part was a lie or not. I wasn't kidding myself that getting along with Grandmother would be easy. Only I knew, if I lived with her, I'd have to see to it that good things happened to me.

When Grandmother came to get me, and after I had my junk packed in her car, I said good-bye to Dad and Monica and Cindy. Monica stayed pretty much in the background, but Cindy hopped around, asking if she could move into my room. I said I didn't care, but Dad gave her a firm no.

He wanted it waiting for me in case I came back for a visit.

Grandmother stopped at the school so I could run in and get my withdrawal form. Everyone gathered around to give me hugs. Even Ruth came out of her office to wish me luck. Stacy and I held hands as she walked me down to David's room. "In just a couple of years," I told her, "we can have an apartment together."

David met me at his classroom door and bear-hugged me good-bye. When he let go, he pointed across the courtyard at TJ, who was standing by himself, smoking a cigarette. I shook my head and started for the parking lot, until my heart stopped me. I crossed the courtyard and stood in front of TJ, real close. He stiffened.

"I won't mess your head up again, TJ, but"—I took the cigarette out of his mouth and dropped it on the ground— "you should know you're the only boy this chickie's ever cared about."

I stood up on my tiptoes and kissed TJ. One last sweet kiss. And I turned and left Cooperation High.